THI

A NOVEL

THE DREAMER

A NOVEL

BY

LESLIE GRUBER

www.bookstandpublishing.com

Published by
Bookstand Publishing
Morgan Hill, CA 95037
3720_2

ISBN 978-1-61863-352-1

Printed in the United States of America

CHAPTER ONE

The seeds of my overwhelming desire to escape from my own country were sown in the exhilarating fall days of 1956. The fateful day was the 24th of October. I woke up with a start on that memorable morning to my mother's gentle shaking. Her worried face hovering over me gave my heart a lurch. I sat up and looked out the window: a sullen, grey Budapest morning greeted me. I expected just another dreary day at school, but this was very much out of the ordinary. By now my mother should be fighting her way onto crowded streetcars loaded with morose, tobacco- smelling people, all on their way to work.

"I won't let you go to school today. There is fighting on the streets," she said, standing by the window, peeking out.

"What do you mean fighting? Who is fighting?" Suddenly fully awake, I was out of the bed, breathless with excitement.

"Young people. Students and workers. It started last night. All I heard is that a crowd demonstrating at the Radio building were gunned down. Then they stormed the army barracks, the Hungarian soldiers opened the arsenals and now this has turned into a full scale revolt. They're fighting the Secret Police and Russian tanks. I heard this from Bandi, who just came home to eat something"

Bandi was our neighbour's son, a university student.

Just to prove my mother's words, a staccato of machine gun fire erupted somewhere near-by. A chill ran down my spine.

The radio was on:

"Citizens of Hungary, comrades! Last night armed counter-revolutionary elements, aided by imperialist forces from outside the country clashed with our security forces. The workers' and peasants' government asked our fraternal brothers in the Soviet Union to help eliminate these gangs of armed bandits who're fighting against the legitimate government of Hungary. The minister of the Interior declared amnesty for any person who lays his arms down by midnight tonight. Anyone found with a weapon after this deadline will be dealt with by summary execution."

1

The stern baritone of the announcer, so familiar from days before, had a sound of desperation to it. Then a very popular soccer commentator came on, trying the voice of reason, urging the rebels to lay down their arms, and promising amnesty. This was clearly earth shattering stuff. This couldn't be happening. I should be sitting in a Russian language class, restless, bored, hating every minute of it. This could not be real. Every cell in my brain was protesting against this intrusion to normalcy.

Shivering in my pyjamas in the unheated room, goose bumps on my skin, I also looked out of our window. I saw a crowd milling about, aimlessly forming impromptu discussion groups.

"Í have to go out Mom, find out what's happening. All my friends are there." I tried on a voice of fearless maturity, but it didn't come out well. She knew I was just a scared boy.

Already knowing she couldn't hold me back, my Mother embraced me, holding me tight against her frail body and pleaded: "I don't like you going out there. I lived through the siege of this city in '45, the killings, the shelling, the bombs falling from the sky. You were just a baby, you don't remember. I lost your father, I raised you by myself. You're the only one left, you're my life. What if something happens to you?" Seeing my discomfort, she let me go. She wringed her veined hands in distress.

"Mami, all my friends are out there. I promise I won't go outside of our street."

"Eat your breakfast at least. Who knows what we'll be eating next if this fighting keeps going on."

My Mom could see there was no way she could keep her 14 year old son locked up when such a colossal event was taking place. After repeatedly promising her I wouldn't go beyond our street, I skipped breakfast, went out the door in a flash and joined the throng.

Once I stepped outside of our building, as I looked around and sniffed the air, something monumental happened inside my head. My world shifted; I entered a new dimension. My familiar, miserable but secure life sunk beyond the horizon. This was a weekday morning; the street should've been empty, everybody working. Instead it was full of

2

excited people in fluid motion like a human wave sloshing against the walls. The crumbling facades, the broken pavement, the gritty smoky air was the same but the promise of unpredictable, uncontrollable events was in the air. All the certainties of the past seemed disintegrating. The iron grip of the State, once unchallengeable, disappeared overnight. The balloon of my spirit soared to the sky. It was the feeling of freedom, a feeling I'd never felt before.

To the South the oil refineries were on fire and the already dark skies were blanketed with a grief-black shroud. The air smelled of burning oil, forever engraving it in my mind as the odour of calamity. Even today, when I get a whiff of burning diesel anywhere, those desperate days come back haunting me through the forgotten decades.

The brooding sky was a forewarning of the horrors to come.

I joined my playmates, all highly agitated by all the happenings. Our droll, boring lives got a mighty jolt. This wasn't some picture we watched in the smelly neighbourhood movie-house; this was a live action show. This was fun. Flaunting parental warnings, we freely mingled with gun carrying youths, scouting the neighbourhood for possible trouble spots.

As the day wore on, rumours swept through the crowds. We were aimlessly loitering outside our building, passing to each other one fantastic tale after another, when suddenly a Russian tank turned a corner and everybody ran for cover. I jumped into the doorway of our building along with our fat caretaker, peeking out at the tank rattling on chained tracks when suddenly it burst upon our building a heart stopping salvo. Fortunately it was aiming above our heads at some Molotov-cocktail throwing youths. Naturally, we both jumped back, scared to our core, and promptly got stuck in the doorframe. The big, bacon-fattened super and the skinny kid were wedged solidly in, unable to move while the clanking steel monster slowly closed in on us. We wriggled frantically for our lives when finally our clothes gave way and by ripping fabrics and tearing buttons we burst free just in time for a dash to the bomb shelter. I never had a more frightening experience since then, when that sixty ton of menacing steel was grinding its slow way toward me, the roar of it's engine and that hideous grating sound of the tracks echoing in the walled-in narrow street.

As the fighting intensified, we spent the next ten days in the bomb shelter, lucky to have one. The city turned to rubble around us.

3

First we tried to sleep in our beds, but the constant hammering of machine guns in the terror-filled nights drove us down to join the other tenants.

We lived in the centre of the uprising. The Kilian Barracks, the headquarters of the rebels was only a couple of blocks away. There was no food, heating, electricity. We had no beds in the unheated shelter so all of us tried to sleep on chairs.

We were living in the twilight zone for ten days. Those ten days were all the Hungarians managed to live in freedom before the Russian juggernaut came back with a vengeance and smashed our short-lived liberty. The fighting was fierce, public squares filling up with makeshift graves, covered with flowers. I saw a burned out Russian tank, the crusty, blackened corpses of the soldiers scattered in every direction, the ribs sticking out from crushed bodies.

These were feverous, adrenaline fuelled days. I saw things no fourteen year old should ever see. The dead freedom fighters were so small, insignificant, lying by the curb like abandoned packages. The brown patches of dried blood had no relations to the red stuff coursing through our veins. The drifting clouds of brick dust from collapsed buildings mixed with the smell of cordite and burning oil from exploded tanks were the smells of this revolution.

Near our building was a big flour mill, and one of our neighbours went to fetch a bag of flour, so we could bake some bread. He was gunned down, and he lay there on the top of the big white sack for days, his blood etching a dark scar onto the white cloth then running down in rivulets onto the pavement. Draught horses were the only meat supply, and when they were inevitably shot, some brave soul carved meat out of them during a lull in the fighting. What shocked me more than dead humans were the leftover parts of the abandoned carcasses. I saw a horsehead by the drainage grate with a horrifying grin of his teeth in his open mouth. It took years to erase this image from my mind. At home we lived mostly on dry beans, lentils and some rice, but were constantly hungry.

In the breaks in the fighting, the streets quickly filled up with people, spreading one fantastic rumour after another. I remember a man running through the streets, yelling:

4

"The forces of the United Nations have crossed the Hungarian border to liberate us!"

Wonderful turn of events, I thought, certain of the verity of the news. People broke out in spontaneous joyful cheers. Then a tank suddenly turned a corner and the crowded street emptied in seconds. The loud chatter of hundreds of voices stopped. The abrupt silence just magnified the sound of the squealing tracks of a T-34 as it rumbled forward, engine roaring, turret swinging until it found a target and with a mighty roar blasted away, breaking windows.

There were many demolished storefronts, but amazingly there was no looting. I never imagined a nation could to come together in a single purpose. The overwhelming, all- encompassing desire to get rid of the Communist yoke united the country.

During those ten short days a remarkable transformation took place. Political parties formed, free newspapers were printed, euphoric editorials celebrating our supposed victory.

After causing much destruction and bloodshed, the humiliated Russians withdrew to their barracks. They were ill equipped for urban guerrilla warfare. The tanks were sitting ducks in the confinement of the old, densely built up city. Many times they couldn't turn their turrets around, and when the cannon got stuck in some doorway or window, the rebels struck. A gasoline filled bottle with a wick burning, smashed into the air intake of the T34 turned the behemoth into a funeral pyre. When the soldiers tried to jump out, our boys picked them off. Later they came with infantry support, but they were easy target for snipers perching on rooftops. After taking devastating losses, the Russians retreated. We thought we'd won.

We kids wandered freely around the ruins, climbed inside the burned out tanks, blatantly ignoring our parents' warnings. On one of our expeditions to a ruined building, advancing cautiously upstairs on a stairway   rising to the next floor with no walls surrounding it, we stumbled into a room to a gut wrenching scene: a corpse of a fighter slumped under a window, grotesquely flinging one of his arms toward us as in greeting while holding a machine gun in his other hand. His face was serene with the resignation of an inevitable fate. One of my mates, out of bravado, pulled the gun from his hand. The body lurched forward, almost falling on his legs. His courage suddenly abandoning

5

him, he screamed and jumped back. He handed the gun to me. It was heavy, menacing, smelling of oil and gunpowder, yet exhilarating, raw power emanating from it's grip. We handed the weapon around, all of us gauging the possibilities of keeping it and using it. Although hardened in the past few days, we were still just kids on the threshold of adolescence, fearful of carrying a loaded gun. So with an unexpressed consensus we put the gun down and retreated from the doomed building.

One day a friend ran up to us, breathless:

"I just saw an AVO guy hanging from a lamppost on Ferenc Boulevard. You guys want to see it?"

It was a frightening but irresistible challenge. No one wanted to appear squeamish. We ran the three blocks to the main street. And there he was, a man hanging from the lamppost by his legs, swaying like a boxing bag, people punching and kicking the obviously dead body. His head wobbled with every hit, his greasy blond hair swaying like a feather duster. From his breast pocket a picture of a woman slid out half way with a smile of a happy day that disappeared forever. He wore the dreaded blue epaulets of the AVO, the secret police. Those days it was the equivalent of a dead sentence.

Then something happened: a new excitement surged through the bloodthirsty crowd. A man in civilian clothes, barefoot and in shorts was dragged toward the next lamppost.

"We caught him hiding in his closet. He tortured me in Andrassy Street 60. I recognize him." a trench-coated man was shouting to everyone. That street address put fear into every Hungarian's heart. It was the headquarters of the AVO, and an infamous torture centre.

The man's face was the palest colour I've ever seen on a human being. It was the death mask of a still living person. The crowd wrestled him onto the ground. Someone produced a length of rope and tied the man's legs together. He didn't move, didn't resist. He knew he was dead. While his legs were roped together, the rest of his body was a free for all. Kicks rained down on this inert pile of flesh, twitching involuntarily at every blow. One handy fellow threw the rope over the loop at the top of the ornamental post, others started to pull. The man rose from the pavement, upside down, doing his death spin.

I had enough. I left my buddies behind and walked home. On my way a desperate longing rose in me. There must be a better place in this world, where the supressed rage, wanton brutality, the hopelessness of this magnitude does not exist. This was the first time the thought crossed my mind: I want to get out of this place, by any means.

Seeing all this devastation, stepping over the dead, seeing the bodies swinging from lamp posts de-sensitized us at this early age. This was education of the cruellest kind. But we were free, a feeling we never had experienced before. The country was free from communist control and we boys were free form parental control. This was a dark euphoria.

The newly formed Revolutionary Government entered into negotiations to withdraw all the Russian forces from Hungary. At the same time the Suez crisis broke out, and to the great misfortune of the Hungarians, suddenly the world's attention was focused elsewhere.

The trusting Prime Minister, Defence minister and his top officials were lured to a Russian garrison outside Budapest under the pretext of negotiating the troop withdrawal and were promptly arrested and eventually executed. Meanwhile the Russian forces were massively reinforced from outside the country, and on the 4th of November they re-entered the city with bloodlust; this time with armoured personnel carriers, a massive number of troops and even bombers.

I remember the cryptic radio broadcast at dawn calling on the forces of freedom to help us. My mother knew better:

"We're doomed Peter" she said. She was no stranger to historic losses, and I admired her stoic calm amidst the great fever sweeping the country.

"It was inevitable. Do you thing the men in the Kremlin will let us get away? Break out of the Warsaw Pact? We are a small, unimportant country. We can't set an example. The Americans will never come to help us. They won't risk a World War for an insignificant little spot on the map".

7

Never have truer words been spoken. She was a realist. Having lived through past horrors she had no illusions.

The hastily organized National Guards put up a heroic fight against the phalanx of Russian armour, but after a few days the fighting fizzled out. The will of the Hungarians was crushed.

I remember one night going up to the top floor of our building to look out over the city. There were no lights, but the sky was painted blood red by the many burning fires. There were the constant ratata of machine guns, the dull thuds of mortar, a black silhouette of a big building suddenly crumbling like a child's sandcastle by the sea. To me this vision was the death-throes of a brave little people.

Then came the nightmare. A state of emergency, curfew at 7pm, martial law, instant execution if found with a weapon, the rounding up of all the rebels, the short-lived National Guards and members of the Workers' Councils. Hundreds of thousands of people fled the country while they could. My mother, seeing no future for us with all hope trampled into the autumn mud, decided to escape too. People were organizing truck transports to the border area all around us. But the drivers asked for a great deal of money, which my mother unfortunately didn't have. So we were left behind to face the frightening, unknown future.

The winter of misery was unleashed upon us.

A drowning nation, surfaced to the air for ten brief days was pushed again under the surface. Then came the dark, silent, endless winter nights. And yet, by morning whitewash signs appeared on walls, calling for a general strike. The country came to a standstill. Big posters in threatening, bold letters proclaimed draconian measures for any strikers. School was out, stores closed and hardly anybody was on the streets. Public transportation was non-existent.

This was a city of two million people without signs of life. The November wind whistled through the rubble strewn streets, the banging of broken windows the only other sound in this frigid city-desert. Hungry, disheartened, there seemed to be no hope, no future, no relief from this season of misery. We were at the limit of our endurance. Nothing to do but sit in the cold room, ponder our standing in the world, listening to the hate-propaganda gushing forth from the radio.

I thought this will never end, but after a couple of weeks of this defiant, catatonic paralysis, as the first signs of life, the temporary graves disappeared from the public parks, streetcars started to run and stores opened. We young kids joined work gangs to clear out all the rubble and re-lay the ripped up paving stones from the barricades. We had no money as nobody worked, and the city offered a small amount for volunteers. Against my Mom's pleading, along with a few of my buddies we enlisted in this dangerous and dirty work, under the watchful eyes of Russian tanks which were positioned on every intersection, their machine guns trained on us. I was a proud boy giving my Mom the few Forints they paid us every night, my first wage I ever earned. We could buy bread and milk after subsisting on beans and rice for a month. But we were still hungry, cold, and bereft of hope. It was a very bleak Christmas in 1956.

By February we were back in school, although a very rebellious, unruly bunch. One of our first acts was to make a bonfire of Russian textbooks, almost burning the school down. For months the black circle on the floor reminded us daily of our defiant act, a refresher to our desperate standing in the world. The teachers were powerless to rein us in.

In another class, a boy volunteered to be the first member in our school of the Communist Youth League. When this news reached us, the leader of our group, who eventually graduated to lead a criminal gang, came up with an idea:

"We should hang the commie bastard up by his neck. Let's go and get him"

Like a pack of wolves, we rushed across the hall and cornered the frightened boy. He was a year younger, a scrawny kid.

"I didn't join in! It's a lie." he screamed and scuffled. Two older boys pushed him against the wall and the third went through his pockets. Triumphantly, he pulled out the evidence, the loathed membership card with the boy's name on it.
"You'll die, you Bolshevik shit!" screamed our leader." His older brother was rumoured to be a wounded fighter, who escaped from the hospital just as the Russians closed in. Now he was hiding, a death warrant on his head. No wonder this boy was bloodthirsty.

One guy took a shawl from a hanger and tied around his neck. He screamed and fought, but there were no teachers around, and we were a force. He was lifted up by two boys and he was hooked on the coat hanger. He twisted and kicked furiously, his face slowly turning crimson. I was sick just by watching this, but was powerless to intervene. I would be next on the hanger. Just then a teacher come by, alerted by the victim's screaming and scattering us, and lifted the choking boy off the hook.

These teenagers were so de-sensitized and full of boiling hatred, they jeered as their prey desperately jerked and twitched on the hook. There were no retributions after. In the atmosphere of insecurity and confusion, when the communists had not yet wholly established their dictatorship, authority was flaunted.

Those who never lived under Communist terror, have no idea about its soul corroding, all- pervasive toxicity. I became aware of the world, came to consciousness during the bleakest of the Stalinist years, the early fifties. My earliest memories are of bombed out buildings, crossing the Danube on a swaying pontoon bridge. All of the eight magnificent bridges spanning the wide Danube were blown up by the retreating Germans, their rusty skeletons bowing into the swirling grey waters with resignation. Façade-less apartment buildings exposing the papered walls and hanging pictures of a former living room three stories high, like a voyeur's glimpse into somebody's life; this was normal for me. Blocks long line-ups for food was a given. Could there be anything different, better? It never occurred to my innocent young mind.

Before I was old enough to be aware of it, I almost lost my mother. If the horrors of the bombing, the starvation, the worry about her new-born baby wasn't enough, her husband died in a motorcycle crash in the midst of the war. My father lost one eye in an industrial accident, thus he was not drafted into the army, to the great relief of everybody. He was an engineer, visiting various flour mills around the country. On one November night he didn't return from his trip. For days my mother had no idea what happened to her husband. Finally someone found her with the news: his bike was hit by a retreating German army truck and he was tossed into the ditch, still alive. Farmers working on a field saw this happen, but there was no ambulance or any kind of help during these panicky, chaotic days when the Russian tanks were just miles away; everybody tried to save his or her own skin. For many days my father lay in that ditch, and not until the front moved on when somebody took the trouble to find an ID on him and somehow relay the message to my mother.

I could just imagine my Mom's aguish: no husband, no food, no income, daily bombing raids and a new born baby to take care of. As she told me, they didn't let her see the body, it was so decomposed. During the funeral service gypsy music was playing on the radio in case an air-raid warning was issued. No wonder she developed a perforated ulcer shortly after. Her pain and fever become so unbearable that my grandma walked for an hour to the nearest hospital to ask for assistance. In the hospital, full of wounded, they promised to send for her the only ambulance on the Pest side of one million people, when they could. Once they made it to the hospital, my Mom on death's threshold, they operated on her in in a windowless OR in February without electricity. She wore her fur coat, gloves and a woollen hat in the ward, subsisting on food my grandma took to her. Once she came home, her weight was 90 pounds.

A few more things must've had contributed to her ulcer: one brother was fighting on the Russian front, from whom they didn't hear from months, another was hiding from the draft. By the time the Russian were closing in on the country, which by the way was the last remaining ally of the Germans, a fascist coup overthrew the government. With the Nazi's help, the Arrow Cross goons, the Hungarian clones of the SS, rounded up every able bodied men, under aged youth, old people for the front. My uncle Feri new the draft notice was a death sentence, so he went into hiding. Next to our apartment building were the cellars of a wine merchant. One end of the vaulted cave was filled up to the ceiling with wine bottles. My Mom, grandma and uncle Feri moved all those bottles a few feet forward, he hid behind them and they restacked them again. Every night my mother snuck into the cellar with food and water and emptied his chamber pot.

This was going on for months. I can't imagine the gut wrenching fear and worry, knowing if someone betrays them, they all could be executed for hiding an army deserter. The Arrow Cross scum were like cornered animals, savagely striking out at everyone, rounding up Jews by the thousands, executing them on the shores of the Danube and tossing the bodies into the river among the ice flows. Army deserters were routinely were shot on the spot. Once the Russians

11

"liberated" Budapest, my uncle still couldn't come out of his hiding place. The roving patrols of the Red Army caught any able bodied man left for "malenki robot" a little work, from where a few returned. Most of them were shipped out to feed the insatiable appetite of the Gulag.

After the situation stabilized somewhat, Uncle Feri came out of his hiding: a wrecked skeleton who never recovered from this ordeal and died an alcoholic a few years later. My mother didn't have a job, and no prospect of getting any, so we lived on money she earned by selling my father's suits, shoes, stamp collection, bartering with country folk, anything to survive. After a year of this uncertainty, facing another bout of hunger and lack of fuel she finally landed a miserable low paying job, a payroll clerk in a shoe factory. These were lean times indeed.

Once I started school, at least there was warmth. My lunch varied between bread with lard or bread with marmalade. Our Budapest neighbourhood had the reputation of being one of the toughest in the city. As we all lived in poverty, we had one outfit for going to school and one for Sunday, one pair of shoes, which we tried desperately to resurrect with shoe polish for the weekend after six days of abuse as combat boots, soccer shoes and footwear for school. For some insane reason the floor planks of the classrooms were saturated with black oil, which was swept up with sawdust daily. Every regularly occurring wrestling match on the floor resulted of our sad clothes getting another rubdown of the wretched black gook, driving our parents to further despair.

Most teachers were very fond of corporal punishments. One's speciality was grabbing you by your sideburns and pulling you up until you were on the very tips of your toes, and upon releasing you, he landed a resounding sharp slap on your face. The red marks of his fingers were visible for hours after. Others resorted to kicking you while you were seated or giving out noogies on the head liberally. Or the most hated punishment of them all, the so called nailer, when you had to bunch your fingers upright while they landed a whack on your fingertips with the big chalkboard ruler.

We returned the brutality in kind. The rooms were heated by stoves. The scuttle, brimming with coal, was sometimes emptied onto the teacher's desk just before he arrived. The resulting epileptic fit and subsequent interrogation, beating and detention never produced a culprit but sometimes conveniently postponed some dreaded test.

One of our teachers especially earned our dislike, since his favourite mode of punishment was silently walking on his gumshoes among us and delivering the worst withering noogies on our heads, out of the blue. On top of that, he taught Russian, the most hated subject of them all. We got our revenge eventually. He was quite a dandy, as much as one could be in those times. One day he showed up in a new pair of dove grey, freshly pressed pantaloons. As he again silently strolled between the aisles, one of our much maligned classmates gave a good healthy whack with his fountain pen from behind, onto his slacks. The next day he wore a different pair of pants and never gave out noogies again.

Our art teacher was a benign old gentleman with a name worth translating: Agenor Beautiful. He came into the classroom, put a vase of flowers or a bowl of vegetables on the desk for us to draw and promptly went to sleep. A brave kid in the first row then proceeded to tie his shoelaces together under the desk. At the back of the classroom stood some big storage cupboards and the hinges on one of the doors were ripped off long ago. This time an accomplice, with a little nudge, dislodged the heavy door, which came crashing down onto the floor with a sound of an explosion. Poor Mr. Beautiful jumped up, or tried to, awakened from his peaceful slumber by the big bang, and promptly wiped out on the floor like a bowling pin, to the great hilarity of our rotten bunch.

Once the new invention, the ball point pen came in to use, the war of spit balls started, often targeting the back of the head of some teacher writing at the blackboard. Female teachers were the exception, since generally they didn't beat us. Our interest in them was more of a carnal kind. The word went around that one particularly pretty young teacher wore no underwear. So we positioned small pocket mirrors on top of our shoes, and tried to look up under her skirt to see what we could see as she walked in the aisles. After a few tries she spotted the mirror and this was the only time the red faced young women gave out a thorough thrashing to the offending boy. Sure enough, she showed up in pants afterward.

Our unruly behaviour was not restricted to the classroom. After school we frequently rode on the couplings at the back of streetcars, crouching low to avoid being seen by the ticket collector. At the stops we pulled on the rope hanging down from the pick-up arm, thus disconnecting the tram from the overhead wires. As the conductor was ready to start the streetcar, we released it up again, to a great explosion of sparks and a crack like a lightning. Then the enraged conductor and sometimes passengers chased us but could never catch us.

The trash was collected by horse drawn wagons. When they stopped to pick up garbage, we put a brick under the wheels from the other side, and the heavy wagon wouldn't move doesn't matter how hard they whipped the horses. We were a brutalized, insensitive generation, the products of the system.

It seemed the poisoning of minds could never start early enough: as young pioneers, wearing the red kerchief, we had endless assemblies, listening to the drone of political indoctrination geared for young, receptive brains. At the end of meetings, we sprung up, and for minutes we chanted: long live Stalin, the supreme guardian of peace, long live his faithful pupil, Comrade Rakosi. The adults were afraid to stop applauding, under the ever watchful eyes of the informers.

The midnight ringing of the bell could mean only one thing: the secret police, the AVO came calling. At the first light of dawn people were relieved that another night passed without an arrest. Why would you be arrested? A denunciation, a casual, careless remark about our leaders, a prominent position in the previous regime, complaints against the constant shortages, praising the capitalist devils, listening to Radio Free Europe, going to church, even wearing an expensive fur coat. You never, ever knew why people around you were arrested and never heard from again.

"People's Educators" came unannounced to every apartment. I remember the shrill, urgent ringing of our bell on one fall evening. As we didn't expect anybody, it was a frightening call. A bespectacled, portly man, with the stern gaze of a believer, strode into our apartment, not waiting to be invited in. His thick glasses made his eyes huge, disorienting.

My mother had already hidden all our pre-war books, displaying works of only the correct kind, the ones my uncle translated from Russian. But the old family crucifix was still hanging on the wall. We didn't have time to hide it behind the picture above it. The man carefully looked around, noticing of course the "religious symbol". He sat down, took out a notebook from his big, black leather case, and started questioning my Mom.

"What do you think about the Fourth Party Congress, Comrade Werner? Do you know the latest figures about the fulfilment of the new Five Year Plan? Do you attend the weekly socialist brigade meetings?"

I sat there, the fear of losing my mother chilling my guts. Then he changed to personal questions:

"What were your parents' occupations in the old regime? How did your husband die? I heard reports that he was an engineer, a reactionary official in the old regime!"

My mother, worn out and small, tried to hold her own, spouting the right answers and more.

"Yes, I do read the Free People". It was the newspaper of the Party (If there ever was a misnomer, an Orwellian doubletalk, a cruel joke, calling the paper Free People).

"I don't go to church, Comrade, don't believe malicious neighbourhood rumours. My son is a squad leader at the Young Pioneers. Look" she said, stepping toward the bookcase with desperate haste, "my brother translated all these Soviet books for the Hungarian masses."

"The Jesus Christ hanging on the wall is an inheritance, an antique left from my grandparents."The stone faced man with the magnified eyes didn't respond.

He started scribbling on his notepad, holding it so we couldn't see what he was writing.
The only sound was the scraping of his pen on the paper.

After about an hour, the big scary man lifted his bulk and left. We didn't sleep much that night. Luckily, nothing happened. Maybe the sight of a broken, grey little widow with her only son didn't qualify her as an Enemy of the People.
At every communist holiday, massive, multi-story portraits were hung from buildings, the ever watchful eyes of Big Brother look-alikes (as I learned many years later from Orwell's book, who I think was one

of the 20th Century's great sages) everywhere, red banners sprouting the slogans of the victorious proletariat, while under them dispirited masses shuffled past, never ever glancing up to read them.

If you sat across from an AVO officer on the streetcar, you froze, didn't utter a word, and hastened to get off the cursed car. One of our neighbours had a midnight visit from the AVO and disappeared for a few years. Nobody knew his whereabouts, not even his wife. We found out later, he got drunk in a tavern and said disparaging remarks about our great leaders. He came back a broken man, never uttering a word about his experiences "inside".

There was a shortage of everything, line ups for essentials, and what you could buy was the poorest of quality. Yet we were told, this was the workers' paradise, our life was wonderful. And you just dare to say otherwise. The capitalists in the West were oppressing and exploiting their people, as we were all to know.

All this I see now by the distance of many years. Going back to my earliest recollections, -although I sensed the adults' fear, oppression and saw the poverty,- I was still a child, a time of blissful shallowness, pursuing a lot more important matters than whatever concerned the adults.

CHAPTER TWO

Our little apartment was our castle where we could retreat from the hostile, threatening world. Inside love ruled supreme. The big glazed-tile fireplace warmed the room, the table was set with simple but tasty food, the radio played some classical music, afterward book reading; it was bliss for a child who knew nothing better. I felt safe then, believing that the harsh reality of the everyday life, the slogans of hatred, the jackboots of communism couldn't penetrate out little cocoon.

I fiercely loved my Mom. On her birthday I decorated the apartment with flowers, wrote my own verses for the occasion. She tried to be stern with me in the absence of a father, frequently using the wicker carpet beater on my behind, which I think I duly deserved. Against the odds, my Mom took me to our Catholic church every Sunday. I liked the atmosphere, the drama of the mass, the majestic sound of the organ, the smell of frankincense. Not the sermon though: I found it boring. My Mom never managed to implant belief in me. I found all the stuff in the Bible just plain unbelievable. I wanted to know, not to believe.

I grew up without a father, but I didn't miss him in my youngest years, not until I saw my friends having fathers. Their strong, reassuring presence, the safety they projected toward any harm that could come to their kids: then I became painfully aware of this void in my life.

I had a father figure though, my uncle who came back from Russian captivity. He never got married and lived with my grandma. He was a talented young classical pianist, who had to give up his dreams, again because of the age he lived in. A job offer at the city hall during the Depression was like a lottery win. So he abandoned his studies and joined the bureaucratic world. He was the one who planted the love of literature, art and film into my young absorbent mind.

Reluctantly he opened up to my relentless questionings about the war and the Soviet Union. After all, he was there and had a first-hand experience. Once he judged me to be reliable and trustworthy, he painted me a picture of unimaginable horrors, human degradation on an epic scale.

"I don't know if you're ready for this, but since you keep asking me, I can tell you I saw things that defy belief. I saw Russian POW's eating the flesh of their dead comrades. I saw partisans hanging from tree branches like huge fruits; I saw trained dogs running under German panzers to blow them up. The Germans shot Russians with outstretched arms and used them as signposts once they froze solid. I could tell you more horrible stories, but I can see you're already too pale."

Once he was captured, he was only a handful who made it back from the thousands and thousands of prisoners. I still remember his solemn, nicotine-ravaged voice, giving me a high because he trusted me with what he said:

"Peter, one thing you have to keep in mind: don't believe what you hear on the radio or in the speeches: the Russian Empire is a dreadful place. People live like animals in earthen dugouts, eat roots and grasses, and have no right to move. They are worse off than they were under the tsars, and that wasn't a picnic either. There is no hope for these unfortunate people. There is not a grain of truth in anything you hear about them. I ask you to remember this."

This was an early wake up call to see things with a critical eye. He was a stern disciplinarian, not given to affection or emotional outbursts, but he planted the seed in me of who I am today.

My uncle had a villa by the Balaton lakeside which he bought before the war. He managed to keep it during the darkest years of terror, because he was a translator of Russian literature, a rare profession of great demand. He learned the language while on the front and in the POW camp. He claimed he needed a peaceful retreat to concentrate on introducing to Hungarian readers the gems of Socialist-Realist literature of the Soviet Union. Thus I spent all my summers at this lakeside paradise. There was no electricity or running water, but a paradise maybe just because of that. No People's Radio broadcasts to reach us, no newspapers, just endless hot days, fresh milk from the local cows and fruit from the orchards.

The fruit more often than not came from excursions of pillage with my cousin. We raided the cherry, apricot, and peach trees in the neighbourhood as they came to fruition, often running for our lives as enraged peasants pursued us. This was one of the age-old delights of a true childhood.

18

The villa had a shady veranda supported by white pillars, the perfect place for discussions of politics late into the night, in the dark, in hushed tones with trusted friends and neighbours. Nobody could hear us, there was no danger of informants around. During these long sessions, listening eagerly to the adults, I came to the realization that all that I was hearing outside of our house were lies. There was a better world out there. Our life wasn't the wonderful utopia we were told we were building. I also learned that life before the communists wasn't as terrible as they taught us. There was meat and butter in the stores then, no line-ups for bread, toilet paper or anything else. People were not dragged out of their bed at midnight on trumped-up charges. Before the war, even if it wasn't a full democracy, it was a civil society with rule of law. Nobody could be declared an Enemy of the People and shipped off to a concentration camp.

For a child, whatever he grows into, it's the norm, his reference point. He or she never questions the status quo on his own. By eavesdropping on the adult discussions during these night sessions, the first cracks on my young mind-set appeared, widening quickly. The freely flowing ideas and opinions converted me to a non-believer, a sceptic of everything I would hear outside my family. My cousin and I were warned against saying anything about what we heard there, to anybody, ever.

The water was from our well, lighting was by kerosene lamps. We lowered balls of watermelon and cantaloupe into the deep well: this was our refrigeration. For milk we biked a long way to a farm where we watched as the woman of the house milked the cow, giving us the frothy white liquid still warm.

A small chapel stood on the shores of the lake wedged between holiday houses. My Grandma took me there every Sunday for mass. The railway station was just above the chapel on a rising. Every weekend so called Vanguard Workers' trains transported the worthy of socialist labour to the lakeshore for a day's recuperation. As the congregation burst into some soul lifting hymn, the workers on the idling train above us tried to overwhelm us with their communist marching songs. This contest of beliefs, ideologies kept on going until the train moved on. I thought it was hilarious; they couldn't do anything form high above us to shut us down, could only try to shout us down.

The lakeshore was lined with stylish, opulent summer houses of the well to do of the old regime. The communists confiscated them all, and now they were "relaxation houses" of various factories and institutions. Only the faithful got the coveted two weeks in one of these lovely buildings. We didn't realize until later how privileged we were by having our own villa.

I built a perch on top of the big apricot tree in the garden, overhanging the lake and I spent hours gazing at the horizon, trying to decipher what my future would hold. The WORLD was this mysterious, enigmatic universe waiting for me to discover. I read for hours sitting in my eagles' nest any book I could get hold of, preferably from the past. I could be easily distracted from my deep musings though, if I could spot the shapely neighbour girl sunning in her bikini below me. This was the place where I later took my willing girlfriends for illicit trysts.

Once these idyllic summers were over I had to return to Planet Reality in Budapest. I re-joined our neighbourhood bunch of scrawny, up-to-no-good kids. We found a splendid distraction.

The bomb shelter we used during the revolution was built in the early 1940s. This was keeping with the times, as bomb shelters came handy during air raids. It had thick concrete walls, heavy steel doors and no windows. During the Red Army's siege of Budapest in 44-45, it was a lifesaver for the tenants of our building. While people in other buildings lived in rat- infested coal cellars with candles for illumination and no running water, our "luxury" refuge had electricity and sometimes even water.

This I learned from my mother who had lived through those terrifying months. As she told me, she cradled me in her arms on the floor sheltering me with her body, when the allies paid a visit in the sky.

After the war the shelter was abandoned, too airtight for even to mice to reclaim. It was just a dark cocoon containing the memories of past horrors. That is, until we, the new generation of war kids discovered it. It was the perfect environment for close quarter combat. We transformed it into a besieged Stalingrad bunker whose defenders were the few holdouts in the encircled city, expending their last bullets to avenge their fallen comrades. We crawled around on the dirty floor, our wooden machine guns blazing away, the constant 'gunfire' echoing in the empty cavern. We knew the right moves from Soviet war movies. We never ran out of ammunition, were never wounded. What a great time we had.

As the years piled on each other, we found other uses of the bunker. Puberty started to stir up our bodies (as well as our souls). All of a sudden, we looked differently at our girl playmates. With keen interest, we noticed the timid mounds sprouting on the girls' blouses, their behinds nicely rounding out, their voices switching to a flirtatious pitch, nylon stockings replacing socks. They in the most part were not unfriendly toward our awkward advances.

Then came a time when our frequently fought over dungeon served again a very useful peacetime purpose. An old mattress on the floor, some candles, blankets and the seducer's boudoir was ready. Its existence ignored or forgotten by parents, it was the perfect hideaway to take the girls for some exploratory anatomy lessons. It was concluded that we were both teachers and students in this age old play of discovery. All girls were rated, based on how far one could go with them. Of course a great deal of exaggeration took place describing our encounters; consequently nobody could be sure at the reliability of these ratings. I can only speak for myself.

Magdi was the oldest and most learned of our group. She was already going out with bigger boys, even men, but she didn't lose her benign interest in her former playmates' sexual well-being. Whenever I had a chance, I lured her downstairs. She was a willing partner, and today I'm certain I could have gone "all the way" but in my timid inexperience I satisfied myself with fondling her silky firm breasts with sweaty hands while breathlessly kissing her cherry mouth. I can still recall her face of mild disappointment when we finally surfaced from the depths, my whole body thoroughly wringed out by unfilled desire while she climbed the stairs ahead of me, her hips swaying with deliberate slow rhythm. She gradually drifted away from our circle; the call of the street was too strong for her. Poor Magdi was seventeen years old when one day she took some sleeping pills, lied down on their kitchen floor and opened the valves on the gas stove. Nobody really knew why she killed herself; she was on her way to become a full time professional, maybe she saw what her future had in store.

I was left in search of other willing partners. Juli was my next target in my libido-driven scheming. To begin with, she was much harder to lure down to the dungeon of forbidden desires. She claimed her mother had told her not to do anything with boys, let alone lock herself inside a bombproof bunker. But her long and silky auburn hair, her summer dress revealing some very promising contours, the golden fleece of fluffy hair on her long suntanned legs made her hardeningly attractive. I tried and tried with lust driven determination, when finally I stumbled upon the key to her.

It was money. Well, this created a seemingly insurmountable obstacle as I had no money or any prospect to earn some. Boys who bought her ice cream, contributed to her paper napkin collection, and better yet, gave her money, found her more agreeable. The situation called for desperate measures: one of my older, streetwise buddies suggested that I sell some of my mother's books. As I mentioned earlier, all the pre-war books were hidden in the back rows of the bookcase. Many of these were banned by the Communists as bourgeois trash, therefore in high demand on the black market. Certain shady underground booksellers were willing to pay good money for these. Of course the "good" money was but a fraction of what they charged to eager buyers. My partner in crime happened to know such a guy, having sold many of his own parents' books to him. So we stuffed my schoolbag full of the contraband from the back rows of the shelf and sold them to the book shark. After my friend took his commission off, I was still left with what seemed to me a big sum of money. Thus the road was open to the delights of Juli.

I wasn't sure what I could buy to dazzle the object of my desires, so I asked her.

"Well, now that you have money to buy stuff for me, don't bother with it, just give me ten Forints and I will buy what I like." She threw her hair back and swayed her hip.

This was a hefty sum for me but my urges swept away any financial considerations. I handed her the money and finally we were heading down to the cellar. In this tender age I didn't grasp the concept of prostitution and found a fair price to pay for the pleasures awaiting me. I decided to be bold and go farther than with Magdi, boosted by tales of conquests by back alley Casanovas. She let my hand slide under her blouse and she returned my eager kisses, but the below-the-

22

waist department was closed off. Hard as I tried, she expertly shooed away my surgical hands. Half demented by lust, I eventually asked her why she fought off my scouting missions toward the South. Obviously she ignored her mother's warning, so what is this devious game playing?

"You can do more if you have another ten Forints," she breathed out softly, flipping her long eyelashes over her china blue eyes.

This shameless exploitation of the sexually deprived registered only vague uneasiness as I had more money and she was right there, reclining half undressed in the candlelight like some teenage Maya, her hair a cascade of velvet.

"I will give you the ten after, I promise," I pleaded, but she wouldn't let any more advancement until she had the money in her greedy little hands. Naturally I ended up giving all my money to her without the ultimate goal achieved. Although we were the same age, she was more mature, as girls tend to be at this age, experienced the ways of the world, and as they say, knew a sucker when she saw one.

Totally flustered, penniless again and facing the prospect of my mother discovering the missing books, I decided Juli was not worth pursuing. Fortunately the calculating little vamp couldn't tease me for long as they moved away and I never heard of her again.

One of my friend's mother worked in the Party Propaganda Institute. They received western magazines, which were kept under strict control. Ivan's mother smuggled these home from time to time, risking her job and maybe even jail. Ivan let me see them when she wasn't home. Time, Life, Look, the German Stern, and Paris Match were the ones I recall. Through these glossy, full colour pages a door opened to a Magic Kingdom for me. Especially the American publications stunned me: Could there be such a place where all this was possible? Incredibly sleek, streamlined cars with beautiful young people sitting in them were driving toward stunning scenery. Kitchens of unimaginable modernity, with a pretty smiling housewife making dinner with gadgets I had no clue what their purpose was. There were refrigerators the size of armoirs, bursting with tantalizing food. I didn't know until I saw them that there are such things as *colour* televisions. We were getting five hours a day of black and white programming on one channel then.

I didn't understand the text of course, but it didn't matter, the pictures told the story. From chocolate bars to tooth paste, from transistor radios to jewellery, from sunglasses to cereal, they were all so good looking, enticing, desirable. And the tobacco ads: handsome men offering sleek, filtered cigarettes to beautiful models in skimpy clothes in fabulous settings. Airlines offering the world at your feet: shiny jet airplanes cutting across always blue skies, smiling stewardesses offering drinks to happy passengers thirty thousand feet up in the sky. I wasn't so naïve as not to realize that all this was advertising, an idealised image of the world. But still, they proved beyond doubt the existence of such products and such services.

To reinforce these illusionary pictures, hard evidence surfaced to prove it beyond doubt the delights awaiting to someone entering these western wonderlands. A relative of ours visited us from America, a refugee of 56, who were now allowed to come back and spend some much needed dollars.

He showed us colour photos of his swimming pool in his backyard, a bar in his basement, a garage with two chrome wonders. If this wasn't enough, then he told us that he can heat his house with just a touch of a dial and warm air comes though the floor. He had two colour TV's, one in his bedroom. He keeps steaks and roasts in his freezer. His wife didn't need to work, she was a staying home mother. He wasn't some kind of a millionaire, just a house builder. He was a braggart, no doubt about it, but still, all he said and showed us was true beyond doubt. This hard proof totally threw me off. Here was a living, talking person, in clothes made in the USA, wads of cash in his wallet, taking Polaroid pictures of us which miraculously developed in front of our eyes. This guy was from another planet.

My desire to get out of Hungary was reinforced by seeing through these newly opened windows to this different world. If I could get out, I knew where to go. The old seed which was planted in me during those horrific days during the revolution was watered by my constant search for clues and evidence of life in the West and grew into my solid tree of purpose. Maybe this was the first impulse to start me on the long road which led me to my life today.

CHAPTER THREE

Then the sixties came upon us, a decade of monumental change. If a person in 1960 could foresee how the world will look like at the end of 1969, could not believe his /her eyes or ears.
The British still ruled over most of their restless empire. Martin Luther King was an unknown preacher in a black church. The peasants of divided Viet Nam went peacefully about their labours. Mick and Keith were scrawny teenagers listening to old blues records. Paul, John and George just formed a band, the Quarrymen. The ghettoes of Detroit and Los Angeles were still standing.

But the whiff of change was already in the air: on the new media, television, a young, Catholic, Eastern Establishment candidate just defeated the sweaty, shifty Richard Nixon wearing a five o'clock shadow. An oily southern kid with a strange name of Elvis was already making himself notorious by playing "nigger" music to white kids who went crazy for it. Alas, the world was still stagnant, the calm before the storm.

This decade of change affected my life as well. I could not imagine how or when I could escape from Hungary, but the determination was already there. That by 1967 I'll be back from the Free World was not the part of my feverous fantasizing.

First the awkward business of adolescence had to be taken care of. I hated the technical high school where I had to consider myself lucky to get in. I was interested in books, films, music, and above all girls, not the atomic structure of molecules. I was an indifferent student with lousy marks. My pimply face, suddenly too long limbs, un-cool clothes definitely were not the ingredients I needed to attract girls. The more they ignored me the more intense my longing after them became. I distanced myself from my mother, as we all do at that age. I was terribly lonely. For a couple years my only solace was visiting my father's grave in the cemetery. I still feel sorry for the boy standing in the drizzle among the rows of deserted graves, telling his father he never knew, all his woes, crying. Those were dark days indeed.

Once I graduated somehow, my world brightened up. Just the fact that I don't have to go to that hated school felt like a liberation. I knew there was no chance for me to go to university to study the humanities or film school. Beside my dismal grades, my social background cancelled any chance I might have had. The offspring of the workers and peasants received preferred treatment. My father was an engineer in the old regime and this was a black mark against my name. As the joke went, if you were a peasant child of worker parents, you got in. Or your father was some high functionary in the Party. No meritocracy under communism. Everybody was equal, but some were more equal.

I started to work as a technician in a pharmaceutical factory. The job was dangerous and sometimes deadly. We worked in gasmasks for hours. We had to use rubber boots and brass tools only, as the smallest spark would blow the place to high heaven. The slogan at the factory gate proclaimed proudly:

"In Socialism the Highest Value is Human Life."

I saw two guys burn to death in front of my eyes. They were loading magnesium powder into bags when they just exploded, with only their scorched boots left behind. All the company did was collect money from us for their families.

Despite all this, I kept this job for a single fact: since the work was so dangerous, we worked only forty hours a week when everybody else did forty eight. My weekends were free. There was so much to do, so many girls to seduce, so much beer to drink. I struck up a friendship with two guys, Ivan (the boy who showed me all those western magazines) and Zoli, a mate from high school. Us Tree Amigos formed an iron bond to relentlessly pursue sex, drugs (alcohol) and rock and roll. Our obstacles were many though.

Through some cronies we fell in with the right crowd. There was a semi-underground society of young, like-minded, West-loving youngsters in the city. They formed bands, played in cellars and University Clubs, listened to smuggled-in LPs. We found out about the Beatles and Rock and Roll. We taped the few records endlessly on decrepit, overheating "magnetofons" sometimes cooling them in the fridge. There were three criteria for a good house party: the absence of parents, a tape recorder and booze. So when word got around of a "buli" in somebody's place, we all congregated there. We played all the latest songs we got hold of somehow, not discriminating between Paul Anka or Buddy Holly, Neil Sedaca or Bob Dylan. They were western hits, that was all that mattered. The girls were easy to lure to these parties, and we did our best not to disappoint them.

We tried to listen to western radio broadcasts too. The regime set up huge transmission towers outside Budapest, and jammed the frequencies of Radio Free Europe and Radio Luxemburg. These were the coveted channels to connect us to the mythical West. Late at night we could sometimes hear the latest hits from America and Britain, fading in and out of the ether, giving it an otherworldly, unattainable appeal, like a message from space.

Every Saturday night we lined up outside our favourite clubs, and once inside we were in another world, our world. Getting inside wasn't easy though: the girls could all go in, but in the University Clubs only males with membership were allowed. So we faked ID's, or hid in the toilets for hours before they closed the doors.

One time we gained access through the coal cellar of the building, breaking down the door of the furnace room to get in, arriving with blackened hands. We would do anything to get in: another time, and this is true, we pulled ourselves up in cement buckets from a construction site next door, into a small window of the women's toilet on the third floor, squeezed in to the squealing of the girls, in torn and mortar encrusted suits. But it didn't matter: we were in! To get into one of these big events was a badge of honour.

We all had longish hair (if it was too long, the police stopped you on the street and cut it off right there with rusty scissors); the girls wore miniskirts. There was always cheap beer and wine. The bands played strictly western hits. Some of them became Hungarian rock stars on their own later, once the regime eased off a little. We thought of ourselves as pioneers, listening to these bands before they became big. A little like somebody listening to the Beatles in a Liverpool cellar. At these venues we were sealed off from the sinister outside world so we let ourselves go. Danced like whirling dervishes, drank like sailors, lied to the girls, and snogged in the corners.

We were a select group, maybe two hundred boys and girls all together. We knew each other by sight. We were like a secret society, wearing an invisible badge recognizable only to fellow members. We came from all kinds of backgrounds, but our "outside" life was never discussed. Our bond was the love of rock and roll, the love of everything the West stood for, the common loathing of the regime. Always drunk, we did some foolishly dangerous stunts: mocking renditions of the proletariat's marching songs, reciting vulgar anti-communist verses standing on a chair, wearing Lenin hats or a pince-nez favoured by old Bolsheviks. We were never betrayed. Alas, the truth to be told, we mostly were interested in the girls. Wonderfully short skirts revealing alabaster thighs, fake eyelashes shading promising eyes, fabrics straining against youthful chests, those were the true attractions in these clubs.

Finally I was one of the cool guys. I tried to fix a date for every weekend, possibly with a different girl. The sweaty smooching sessions - usually taking place in some dark park or inside in a corner of a club-very seldom resulted to my ultimate goal. There was no chance to go to a private place for some serious erotica. The home parties were few and far between, and usually just too crowded.

I still managed to chalk up a few conquests, and even fell in love for the first time. I asked this pretty girl, Gabriella for a date at one of these dances, and to my surprise she said yes. My luck held out further because just then somebody who knew somebody invited her for a house party. I was her first lover. I must did something right because I awakened in her a sex crazy tigress. Besides her looks, she was the artsy type, studying to be an interior designer, going to one of the prestigious art schools. This was an extra icing on my snobbish ego cake. We fervently seek out any opportunity for carnal pleasures. She was almost insatiable, and to my virile pride I kept up with her. We ran into troubles too. One sultry summer night in a park, overcome with animal urges, we rolled under a big tree. Once we stumbled out to a lighted street dizzy from an afterglow, to our shock, we discovered that we planted ourselves under a tree shedding some kind of black berries. The back of her dress and my knees and elbows were saturated with black stains. On the long streetcar ride to her suburban house she squeezed herself into a corner and I faced her very close, trying to hide the incriminating evidence. But once she got home, there was no way to explain away the obvious facts. Her parents were not impressed but were pretty easy on her, considering the age we were in.

Cute Gaby eventually discovered that there were many guys, besides me, who were also ready, able and willing to cater to her ever growing needs. She was very honest about it, but when she broke the news, she broke my heart too.

28

After this unexpected blow, I cultivated this self-image of a hardened, cynical cad, who is elevated above emotionally draining attachments. Women didn't deserve love and devotion. How wrong, naïve and untested I was! Anyways, I reasoned, commitment would just hinder my ever increasing urge to escape.

Until I could get out, I still had to give in to my wonder lust somehow. We could travel within the communist bloc, so I set out to visit Poland, the most liberal of the bunch. Hitch-hiking, so called auto-stop was illegal in Hungary, but it was tolerated in Poland. With a friend, we took a train to Krakow and from there on hitch- hiked. Just crawling out of the rubble of the devastating war, the people of this most unfortunate country still welcomed us with warmth. The gorgeous Polish girls were especially friendly toward us. There is a centuries old salt mine near Krakow, about a hundred feet underground. During all those years, out of the salt, the miners carved out an improbable cathedral, all sparklingly white. Under a massive dome, pillars, statues of saints, side chapels with bas-reliefs, all lighted by salt chandeliers and candelabras. It was a magical world, defying belief that such place could exist. It was in this wonderland that I locked eyes with a blond Polonaise with mesmerizing eyes. This mysterious encounter deep under the ground just added to the wonderment of this moment. Her name was Jagusia, The only way to bridge the language barrier was to resort to communication in the hated Russian language. But I didn't care. The ugly words sounded sweet from her mouth. She was from the north of the country, also a tourist. Thus she became the highlight of my tour of Poland, the source of so many fond memories.

I hate to admit, but there were other girls with whom I diligently fostered the cause of Polish-Hungarian friendship. These were welcome diversions from my despised existence while I bid my time 'til my eventual self-liberation.

What was this wretched life I wanted to leave behind? I wake up groaning, despising the light of every day, the devastating hopelessness spreading out to greet me: the walk to the tram stop in the sooty, windswept streets, the shuffling and squeezing into the cold car, inhaling the sour tobacco breaths of the grim masses, the grey unshaven faces, eyes blank, inward turned , leaden with the weights of life. The spark of delight perhaps awaiting me in the evening, the sizzling kiss of cheaply rouged lips, the burn of a strong schnapps shot, maybe a film of consequence, all did little to soothe the now and here. The burning light of escape, the light in the end of the proverbial tunnel was the only ointment on my desolation.

The hopelessness was all around me. The communist world seemed to expand incrementally. They tried to infiltrate and conquer South Vietnam, they established a bridgehead in the Americas in Cuba, they sponsored bloody "liberation " wars in Africa. As I saw it, the blood- red ink of Marxism was flowing across the atlas of the world. And at home, it became clear to me how our society was built on lies. I wanted nothing to do with my country anymore.

To help our heroic Vietnamese comrades, once a month we had to "volunteer" for a so called Vietnamese-Saturday at work, without pay of course. Naturally we tried to do even less work on these days, the bane of my weekends. On top of this imposition, they installed spying Vietnamese "comrades", imported to instil revolutionary fervour into our lacklustre attitude. We hated these little goons, always lecturing us in terrible Hungarian how we don't do enough work, slacking off at every opportunity, and how the cause of world revolution is suffering by this. The little fuckers lived off our money and had an audacity to dump shit on us constantly. This just made me all the more mad at everything this phony system stood for.

The war raging ten thousand miles away disturbed me a great deal. To me the Americans were the good guys. They had to draw the line to stop the ever advancing Red Menace. Nobody else would or could stand up to them as the French's failure before showed convincingly. Yet despite the fundamental righteousness of this fight, the war was unpopular at home, more so by the month. Kids dodged the draft, protested everywhere, wrecked universities, burned American flags. It enraged me to see how, by the waste of thousands of lives, they still squandered the opportunity to stop the communists. I think eventually that war was lost at home and not on the battlefield.

As I stealthily started my research into ways to escape, I didn't get far when a lightning bolt struck me out of my outward looking existence: a draft notice to join the Hungarian People's Army. But bad news loves company: on the same day there was shocking news in the papers: President Kennedy was shot. These were dark November days.

My lovely, semi-long locks were sheared to my skull as I reported to the designated recruitment centre in the city. We had no idea where would we be going, secrecy being the main preoccupation of the army. An amicable, casual atmosphere ensued there. A handsome, athletic young lieutenant gave a speech:

"Dear Comrades. You are about to join the glorious People's Army to fulfil your sacred duty to the Motherland. This is a highest honour a young man can achieve. You'll learn discipline, devotion to duty. We'll teach you how to handle your weapons, how to fight. You'll grow to hate your enemy, the warmonger, imperialist oppressors of the working classes....."

The speech went on for a while, regurgitated the same sloganeering we heard from so many sources during our short lifetime.

We had coffee and cakes. Then a fleet of buses took us to the train station, accompanied by friendly sergeants. During the long train ride to a distant provincial town, we tried to make friends, consoling each other: this doesn't look as bad as we had heard.

We arrived after midnight. Torn away from our families, out of our cosy environments, hell's gates opened and our old life disappeared into the dark night. In the cold drizzle, the friendly sergeants turned into screaming beasts. We were corralled into squares, and marched off toward the barracks like cowed lambs. There a finely tuned concert of abuses, insults and threats greeted us in the foulest language the Hungarian mind can produce. We were stripped naked, and ushered into showers: the shuffling crowd of bald headed naked bodies herded into shower rooms brought up horrific images of the Holocaust. After a short sprinkle, a good dosage of DDT powder was shoved up in our asses and into our armpits, making sure we got a handful into our faces too. Next came the dressing up. The second year soldiers just threw any size boots and tunics at us. It was our job to find the right size and exchange it with someone. The loud concert of unceasing screaming made us more confused, frightened, and lost. By the time we got to our straw filled mattresses it was after 2am.

A roaring call to get up dragged us out of our troubled, very short sleep. It was 5:30 and dark outside. The rhythmic thudding of hundreds of boots running below on the parade ground in the black night sounded like the drumbeat of Armageddon. In no time we joined the throng, shivering in the frosty air, running and jumping until our breath gave out. The constant shrill howling of the drill sergeants urged us on until near collapse. Push-ups on the sheet ice of the ground; if you didn't do it fast enough, they kicked your hands apart so you experienced a very unpleasant face plant into the ice. That was when I received frost bite on my hands: they swelled up, and the skin peeled off. The doctor in the infirmary said it'll heal on its own. For years afterward I felt the weather changes in the joints of my hands, reminding me of the awful times in the Army.

After this nightmarish morning things didn't improve. Around the clock, non-stop harassment, running, washing floors, and cleaning toilets was the order of the day. Short breaks for awful food - which we gulped down like hungry wolves- then back to guard duty, weapons inspection and all that. Militaries around the world are doing basically the same thing: break down the personality of the soldier, wipe out his independent thoughts, and turn him into an obedient, unthinking robot. But in Hungary, in 1963, shortly after the doomed revolution, the fierceness of the regime's attitude toward us was a clear indication of the desire to break us, grind the youth of the next generation into an obedient mass. Well, they didnt succeed completely.

The Army with fiendish logic selected the drill sergeants from the countryside, the poor, uneducated, surly lads full of resentment toward us city kids. Therefore they did their loathsome tasks with enthusiasm and vigour. Even the officers were of the right "cadre" of men, promoted for the only criteria: they were from the proper background: worker or peasant.

Sometimes we had our secret sweet revenge: a political commissar of little education, he harangued us about the evils of capitalism, imperialism, the misdeeds of President Johnson or Robert McNamara or Dean Rusk. Except he pronounced it Yonshon , Emseenamara or Dhe-an Roosk, pronouncing the names phonetically, as an ignorant Hungarian would. So we politely answered his questions, pronouncing the names back to him likewise, while the rest of the platoon tried not to die of suppressed laughter.

We were a badly trained, unwilling force, absent of any motivation. The enemy would've had an easy time with us. All we did was marking time, like inmates in a jail. We stole food at any chance we had, dodged duties, sometimes went AWOL for days, got drunk at any opportunity. I never felt more the total bankruptcy of this regime than in the army: there was no hope for this system to succeed. I think we were more dangerous to the People's Army than any enemy could've been. It was two years of a wasted young life.

Luckily I found a soul mate among the rookies, a fellow traveller if you will, Laszlo. His father was a doctor, an art collector, so he came from a cultured, protected environment. He suffered greatly by all the brutality unleashed upon us. A soft-spoken, slow-moving, dreamy boy, he stuck out of our rough bunch. He and I almost automatically struck up a friendship which lasts to this day.

To ease the grimness of our ordeal, we dreamed of escaping to the West, laying elaborate plans to get out. In the meantime, we listened to the forbidden radio stations (especially dangerous within the Army)on my transistor radio under our blankets after lights out, transporting ourselves to the mythical land of plenty and free; Bob Dylan came to our dark cocoon like a rolling stone.

The rare occasion when my buddies or old girlfriends were allowed to visit me just made my heart ache more, for they give me a glimpse into my dear, forgotten, previous life. I also had to endure the jealous ire of the hick sergeants afterward, because of my fashionable girlfriend, and long-haired, blue jeans-clad buddies. Seeing these people identified me as one of the "West Worshipping" urban sophisticates.

Laszlo and I never joined the KISZ, the Communist Youth League. We were the only two in the whole platoon, and when the rest of them marched off to some indoctrination session, we repaired to the canteen without fail. Somehow we were never harassed to join, maybe it was just too obvious we didn't belong there.

Many young men ruined their health trying to get an exemption. Some drank litres of vinegar to have a terrible stomach ulcer afterward. Some drank so much coffee before examination they ruined their heart for good. Such was the dread of serving in the People's Army. Others couldn't cope with the constant bullying and unceasing exhaustion, the relentless strain of the Army life. One of our quiet, unassuming comrades shot himself in the head while on guard duty. One tried to escape with his weapon, was captured shortly, and in a show trial in front to the whole regiment he received a sentence of twenty years in a punishment battalion.

Once we earned leave, the outside world in the small provincial town didn't promise much. The girls were considered cheap sluts if they associated with soldiers. So we counted the days 'til the end like prisoners do.

Second year in the Army was more bearable. It was our turn to abuse the new recruits, let them do all the dirty work. We did some stunts that still make me smile to this day. One morning we carried the bed of our drunk, sleeping comrade's to the toilet. He didn't wake up until an officer, no less, went for a pee and found the private snoring contentedly in the stinking room. He had a rude awakening indeed, absolutely confused and waddling around in his barefoot on the piss drenched floor, having no excuse and no idea how he got there.

We were at a summer training camp, where, as was the rule, we got drunk at every opportunity. We formed a kind of "rock" band with some of our fellow soldiers who had some musical training. I latched on as a "roadie", so I can do the tours with them to neighbouring villages and bask in the attention of peasant girls and treated to massive amounts of food and wine. One of my friend, who trained to be an opera singer and later became the member of the National Opera House, started the rendition of the old Italian standby, O Sole Mio, but the accompanying accordion player was so drunk he broke into the Memory of Sorrento, another Italian song. The sophisticated crowd of cart drivers, tiller men and swine herds didn't notice anything amiss until the accordionist, less and less resistant to the pull of gravity, slowly keeled over and buried himself under his instrument. After this disgraceful performance we stumbled back to camp. As I lay down, the tent started to turn around and around until, in a panicky urgency of the need I heaved into one of the boots lined up at the entrance. I fall into unconscious sleep right away and I didn't open my eyes until I heard a mighty roar: our sergeant just put his boot on. No need to describe his rage and bloodthirsty revenge seeking, but I was the only one who knew the culprit, and for sure I wasn't going to say anything.

All my escape dreams were on hold, I was dying to get out but time moved like honey on a cold day. Laszlo and I sat in the barrack mess hall, drinking warm beer, counting the days, hours, plotting and fantasising about how and when we'll get out. There was not even a second of hesitation about this. Not going was not an option.

At the age of 22, I finally was let go from the military. Then the most curious thing happened: I had a hard time adjusting back to civilian life: I was longing for my buddies, the jokes, pranks, dirty talk, and the camaraderie.

I started to pursue girls again, to make up for the two years deficit I spent in the Army. I changed jobs to a less hazardous one, a sedate, time wasting excuse. I tried to hook up with my old friends, but they drifted away, having steady girlfriends, establishing careers, something I didn't want to hear about. We still met occasionally, but females were in the picture now, and as always the case, were driving a wedge between us. Just as well, since my mind now was on the business of getting out of the "big jail". If I wasn't dead serious about it before, one defining event a few years later firmed up my plans.

In the summer of '66, the underground information network (word of mouth really) spread the news of a so called Hippy Jamboree at Lake Balaton. All "happenings" were happening at the lake in summertime. The best bands played in outdoor venues, all the "hip" kids hung out. The date was set, and sure enough a bunch of us joined the crowds filling the trains.

We arrived to this small resort town, wearing our most precious, diligently faded jeans and colourful shirts, trying to imitate the western kids. On the bandstand in the main square a brass band of stout older men were playing martial music, despised by us, of course. One of us produced a couple of lemons, just for this occasion. We cut them into segments and started to lick them in earnest, right in front of the hard blowing band. Just try to imagine for a minute someone licking a piece of lemon: your salivary glands go overtime, more so if you can see it happening in front of you. As it was inevitable, the hapless musicians filled up their instruments with saliva in no time, giving out hideous and tortured sounds. They fought their way through their piece, but someone must have sent for the police. A van pulled up and two cops bundled the four of us into it. I was with my current girlfriend, a dress bursting stunner, whom I didn't know well but had high hopes for her (and me). Two other friends were our partners in crime.

As they led us into the town police station, our cockiness quickly dissolved. A building erected to instil fear: the totalitarian regime's first stage of crushing dissent. Long, cold corridors echoing with every banged door like a rifle shot, shrill hard voices reverberating through the walls. They made us wait for a long time, sitting on a hard wooden bench. We had hours to contemplate our options, bemoaning of all the action we would be missing, just stewing in our uncertainty.

Finally they led us into an office: one desk, harsh overhead lights, and two policemen. They took our wallets, emptied the girl's purse and one Neanderthal-looking cop started to search us, patting down our bodies with practiced efficiency. After the boys, he proceeded to fondle my girlfriend, slowly feeling up all her lovely curves. She was obviously frightened and disgusted, and protested feebly. When he reached her thighs, she burst into tears. I was scared to my bones, but felt I had to say something.

"Don't do that, please, she is just a young girl, nothing to do with this."

The cop stood up, turning, he appraised me with a condescending look and landed a tremendous slap on my face. The force of the unexpected hit propelled me across the desk next to me, upending a big inkwell onto a bunch of paperwork. This incensed the ape man very much.

"Look what you have done, you filthy hooligan. Destroying state property? Spoiling important documents? I'll teach you! Stand up, you piece of shit!"

I scrambled on to my feet when with casual brutality he kicked his black boots into my groin. The lightning shock of dense, unbearable pain shot up to my brain, and I must have given out an animal howl. As I bent over my crushed testicles he gave my face a sharp knee-up, crushing my lips against my gums and ripping my nostrils. As I writhed on the floor, the strong brute jerked me up by my hand and pushed my palm onto the ink soaked desk.

"We'll have your finger prints taken."

As he said this, he unbuckled his truncheon - what we called Kadar salami, after the boss of the Communist Party- and started to swing it with apparent glee. He was ready to crush my fingers. We were at eye level. I looked into his small, excited eyes, seeing cold, merciless hatred. Hatred of everything we stood for: our trendy clothes, our lovely, easy girlfriends, our city accents, hatred of knowing he could never be one of us. He wasn't much older, in his late twenties, but already well-practised in the police brutality. Just as he was ready to break the bones in my hand, the door opened, and an officer walked in. He must have heard my scream of agony. The other, younger cop, who didn't say or do anything during all this snapped to attention, while my tormentor let my hand go and lowered his billy club.

"What's going on here?" he asked in a reprimanding tone. The bully immediately switched to cop talk:

"We apprehended these individuals at Kossuth Square, Comrade Lieutenant. They were behaving in a hooligan-like manner, licking lemons in front of the Workers' Guard band." I thought I saw an almost undetectable bolt of humour in the officer's eyes, but his face remained stern.

This was bad news. The Workers' Guards were the armed wing of the Communist party, not to be messed with. It was a collection of misfits widely feared, given a licence of lawlessness. Every totalitarian regime needs their devoted armed thugs, just like the Nazis had their SA and the Italians their black shirts. This could mean trouble beyond mere beating.

But then my buddy, Miklos spoke up. During all this time my friends stood mute, frozen to the floor in fright, my girlfriend whimpering softly and gasping every time I was hit. I didn't expect any sound out of them, after what happened to me. But Miki, as we called him, bravely piped up:

"We are innocent vacationers here comrades, and we don't deserve this kind of treatment. My father is the Secretary of the Party in the Ninth District of Budapest, and a firm upholder of socialist legality. I'm sure he will look into why you treated my friend this way."

This threw the officer off. He glanced at the bully, and picked up our documents, examining them. I admired Miki's audacity: his father had nothing to do with the Communist Party, he worked in a bank. He chose a position high enough to generate fear of reprisal but not so high that a small town bureaucracy would know about him by name. The lieutenant contemplated this for a while. The goon looked pained, examining the ink and blood stained floor. Eventually the officer spoke up:

"Comrade Varga," he said turning to the silent young cop, "escort these people out of the building."

"You," he said pointing toward me, "Stay". As my friends left with urgency, he gave me his handkerchief to wipe the blood off my face, and guided me outside the room. But not before he glanced back to the beater and said in an ominous tone:

"You, comrade Teleki wait for me here."

Outside in the empty corridor he pulled me into a window bay.

"You fell down some stairs while you were drunk and smashed your face into the grate. Do you understand me?" His steady gaze gave away nothing.

"For everybody's benefit, nothing happened here. You better tell your friend not to make trouble. Do you understand?" And I, the crushed little sheep, eagerly agreed. I knew there was nothing I could do. There was no chance to fight the monolith of the terrorist state.

"Go wash your face and the ink off your hand in the washroom, then get out of here." were his parting words.

After I left the brooding, terror filled building, I gingerly eased my throbbing bottom on a nearby bench. I inhaled the sultry air of the summer dusk and convalesced. As I sat there, digesting the happenings of the last few hours, the long, vaguely felt undercurrent of my consciousness crystallized into a rock solid determination: I will get out of this cursed country, leave behind my old life, become free. Even if cost me my life. I never felt so assured and purposeful like this before. Re-invigorated, in pain but full of hope, I set out to find my friends in the dark, suddenly strange town.

Since my face was all torn up, I had to tell everybody the unpleasant experience with a stairwell once back in Budapest. I was pissing blood for days and was very worried about impotency until one morning, to my tremendous relief I woke up with a mighty erection. But I remained impotent in other ways: the helplessness to do anything about my brutal beating, no chance to get justice, to get compensation for my abuse and humiliation.

38

I looked at this Hungarian life as an outsider, with no future in this country, just on a holding pattern until liberation day.

These were also the years when I engaged in my self- education. I went to see all the western movies I could. There was an art-film house, where sometimes, for a few days, they showed Fellini, Antonioni, Truffaut, even Hitchcock movies. These were the nuggets I craved for. The seeds of my lifelong love of films were sown in the dark stuffy bowels of this little movie theatre. In the 60's, Europe was the hotbed of cinematic experimentation, a new, non-Hollywood look at the world. The unsurpassable sexiness of stars like Brigitte Bardot, Sophia Loren, Gina Lollobrigida, Monica Vitti, and the suave, charismatic, strikingly handsome men ,the likes of Marcello Mastroianni, Alain Delon, Jean-Paul Belmondo were the ones we emulated and tried to imitate, Those were the heady days of the emerging new world bursting forth, the world I desperately tried to enter. This was the first time in history, thanks to the movies, when lives lived on a different, more exalted level could be really seen and heard directly, convincingly. The draw of this mystical wonderland was irresistible to me and I dedicated my life to get there.

Books were another link to the outside. The regime started to publish influential western literature, from Sartre to Beckett, Hemingway to Faulkner, Camus to Harold Pinter. These were fetched up instantly but I had my underground book-moles, friendly clerks in the stores who shelved a copy for me in exchange for a few beers in a cellar. I spent most of my meagre surplus money on books, to a great chagrin of my Mom and later of girlfriends who didn't like subsidizing my hobby by paying for drinks.

But the main theme of my life, the escape was on my mind foremost. To cross the Austrian border was a non-starter. This was the imaginary Iron Curtain in real life. Just to go to the border region one needed a special permit. Minefields, electrified fences, trip wires, watchtowers, dog patrols, everything was employed to keep the masses from leaving the workers' paradise. There remained only one possibility: going through Yugoslavia. Although it was a communist country as well, it was not under the Russian yoke: Tito the less harsh dictator allowed it's citizens to work abroad, therefore there was no impenetrable border to Italy. I would have to apply for a special permit, inserted into our internal passport, on a pretext to go to the Dalmatian seaside for a holiday. Word got around, all the way to my ears, how to go across from the divided city of Nova Gorica to Gorizia, Italy.

As I schemed and researched and eventually set in motion the way to escape the country, a girl interrupted the process.

CHAPTER FOUR

Her name was Lily. I still frequented the trendy, semi-illegal University rock clubs, and there it was that I laid eyes on her for the first time.

She stood in the hall, glowing in the halo of her youth and beauty, her reflection shining in the eyes of the boys surrounding her. She was tall, voluptuous and slightly drunk. I stood there a short distance away, under the chandeliers, in the smoke and noise and stared. All her fingers had rings on them, her carmine nails drumming a restless beat on the tumbler. Her free hand ran through her auburn hair, flipping it aside from her eyes, so she could sweep the floor with her regal gaze. She was a queen bee and I was one of the transfixed workers hovering. The music started up, and one of the boys took her to dance. I settled on a barstool, ordered a drink and watched her. She was gyrating her sizzling body to the music, moving elegantly to the rhythm with fake unconcern.

"Dance my lovely, dance," I said to myself. "I know you will be mine one day."

And somehow in my inebriated, dazed state I was certain of that. There were many other pretty, willing, charming girls around, but I sensed: she was different. Those eyes had unfathomable depth, a sensuous whirlpool of desire to pull you down, an unabashed craving for life's gifts. I could not take my eyes off her. I observed every sinuous movement, every flip of her eyelashes, the rippling of calf muscles in her high heel shoes, the swaying of her hair about her face, the tantalizing bouncing of her spectacular breasts. This was something I have never experienced before: I was under a spell.

She was changing partners constantly, boys cutting in one after another. At the intermission, she came to the bar with her partner. Her face was flushed from the heat and dance, her make-up smudged a bit, her green eyes dazzling. Providence or good luck delivered her to the seat next to me. She ordered more drinks, the boy paying enthusiastically. She lit a cigarette, leaving a ring of red desire on the filter. She crossed and re-crossed her legs on the barstool, her sheer stockings giving out a rasping sound like small electric discharges. She turned around and looked at me in a not very subtle way.

"Do you come here often?" I asked. A bad line, but she replied:

"Whenever I can. I like the band, one of the backup singers is my friend." She was communicative.

"Are you with a boyfriend?" I asked. An important question!

"No, at least I can't see any of them right now."

So she is funny. I laughed heartily. She sized me up, a spark of interest in her eyes.

"What about you?" she asked back.

"I try to sneak in here every Saturday."

"No, I mean are you with a girlfriend?"

"Thank God no, otherwise I wouldn't be able to hit on you." She giggled. She turned her back to the guy she came to the bar with and looked into my eyes. A one hundred Volt worth of electricity passed between us. I couldn't hold her gaze long, I started to get dizzy. What was with this girl? I had to hold onto the edge of the bar to steady myself. I wanted to catch her eyes again, to faint into that vertigoes swirl, but she constantly moved, fidgeting with her cigarette, sweeping her hair aside. I wanted her to look at me, so I asked her:

"Would you like another drink?" By this time the payer left the bar with a scowl. She hit me again with those eyes, emptied her glass, had a drag on her smoke, and said with authority:

"Sure. Make it whisky. "

This was my kinda gal - I thought. I engaged her now, we connected, I was on the right track. A boy came to her side and asked her to dance. Without hesitation, she declined him with hauteur. This was a good sign. She took greedy little sips of her drink, her eyes wandering around. I had to keep talking to her lest I lose her. My mind was blank, of course, when I had to be charming, interesting, funny. Time was running out.

"What do you do for a living? Where do you work?" I asked these stupid questions, instantly regretting it.

"Why do you give a shit where I work? Are you with the employment police?"

"No, I'm just curious where such a sharp tongued girl could be found when not in this club. I'm trying to find stuff out about you."

"Please, don't remind me of work. Can you come up with a better line?"

"What about your favourite actor, or film? Better?"

"Not much. Why don't you ask what is my favourite drink?"

"Whisky, I presume. One more?"

"Now you're talking. Yes, make it a whisky"

This girl was a serious boozer. She drinks, smokes, dances, flirts, looks ravishing, what more could I ask for?

"By the way, I love Belmondo and Marcello Mastroianni. Or, actually I would love to love them." She was also the witty kind.

"What are you doing tomorrow then? Can I find a Belmondo movie for the two of us?"

"You're moving a little too fast, don't you think? What's your name anyways?" She was slurring a little, obviously these weren't the only drinks she gulped down that night.

"Peter. And yours?"

"Lily. Lily Nemeth"

"Like the flower."   Looked like my brain had stopped functioning.

"Yes, like the flower," said she with irritation.

The music was loud, people shouting at the bartender; this wasn't a good place to get into serious conversation. Plus my mind was still in a stunned mode. I was actually vibrating with nervousness. I had to say something:

"What is your goal in life? What do you want to be when you grow up?" I asked, knowing this was a stupid question, but she answered with a wit I almost expected from her by now:

"We have a philosopher here, I can see. I don't have a goal. What's the point? Can you get anywhere in this country? Not with my parents' background. I wanted to be an actress, would you believe it? And when I applied for admission to the Academy, you know what they said? We don't need offspring of noblemen in this place. Even before they would give me a chance to read anything. So I work in a cookie factory. Glorious, isn't it. Now you know everything about me." This was brave talk, since she didn't know me from Adam.

"You certainly have the looks to be an actress," I gushed. "You're probably talented too."

"Flattery gets you nowhere, didn't you know this?"

'Starring Lily Nemeth' it sounds good." I continued undeterred.

"Can we close this subject? This is something I try to forget. What is your secret, unfulfilled ambition?

I know there is one."

"You are a perceptive girl. So there is a brain behind those gorgeous eyes."

"Just answer the question."

"OK. Confession time: I want to be a screenplay writer. I want to write movie scripts. That's why I'm working in a chemical factory. To deepen my understanding of the working class. But, bullshit aside, I am in the same boat as you. I couldn't get into any institution of higher education. It's their loss. When I'll be a successful writer in Hollywood, they'll see the error of their ways."

44

"How do you plan to go to Hollywood? You have an invitation by Metro Goldwyn Mayer?"

"No, but I have a plan. Don't talk about it now. Just enjoy the evening, each other's company. Don't go dancing with any guys, just talk to me."

From this time on, I believe events started to run on their predetermined course. A never before felt confidence and self-assurance came over me. I was on a high, outperforming myself. With our last drinks we moved out to the corridor, sat down at a table and started talking in earnest. Small talk progressed into more interesting topics and I was going all the way. I knew I had to impress and charm this girl, and boy did I ever try my mightiest.

As we talked, I inched my seat closer to her. I wanted to smell her fragrance, see her close-up, and hear her sultry voice. All that was missing from a full sensory load was touching her. We talked and talked in that smoky, loud, over-lighted room, all else fading into the background. As discussion topics surfaced one after another, we found ourselves on common ground. While the red ringed butts piled up in the ashtray, our glasses emptied, Lily slowly opened up to me. I'd never met anyone before with so much craving for everything in life. It was intoxicating, on top of all the other intoxicants I had consumed during the night.

When it was time to go, somehow it felt natural to escort her home. She lived only a few blocks away, so we decided to walk. It was an early spring night, full of promise. I was holding her hand. It was silky in a way I never felt skin before. Ever after I referred to her hands as midwife hands, supple enough to handle a new born baby. I was caressing, stroking, and grasping, making love to her hand.

The world receded into the background: there was only her.

The street where she lived was dimly lit, the front door to her apartment building in a dark. Her kiss stunned me for a second. She violently bit into my tongue and lips, her scorching mouth tasting faintly of cigarettes and liquor. Her passion hit me like a tidal wave. Here was a very desirable girl throwing herself at me with abandon, and doing it with all her being.

This was how our love started in that musty, obscure doorway, squeezing her against the peeling stucco, savouring this never before known emotion.

I remember walking from her place that night, through the empty streets, in an euphoric high I didn't know could be felt. I didn't want this night to end. I rode the streetcar for hours, back and forth, gazing at the dirty glass on my reflection, in a tipsy state of my dream world, seeing her eyes behind my closed lids, swaying with the wobbly tram's movement, letting my arms hang down, head lolling, giving myself up completely to this ecstatic feeling. By the time I ambled home, the dissipating darkness with the promise of down marked the time.

I woke up late, curing a headache with my Mom's hearty bean soup. By now she gave up on questioning me about my late night drunken arrivals, knowing she could never get a straight answer out of me. We set up a randes-vous for the afternoon with Lily, and my mind was on nothing else.

We met on Moskva Square, near her place. I was early, pacing up and down, worrying if she will show up or not. My inner feeling was that she was captivated by me too, that I had an impact on her during our long conversation at the club. If she remembered any of it, that is.

She appeared late, giving me a flush of relief. She looked different in the glare of daylight, less glamorous, more everyday, but it just made her all the more real. We were awkward first, being sober and a little embarrassed. But the ice melted fast, and by the time we sat down in a booth with a mug of beer in one of the fashionable beer bars, the electricity was on. She talked and I listened, savouring her whole being while absorbing her words. She told me about her life until we met. It was about heartbreaks, disappointments, boys chasing and harassing her, about the dreadful place she worked, about her parents' love for her, her longing for a better life, for a normal place to live, a meaningful job, for freedom. I liked this. She was talking my language, smoothing the way for me to hit her with my escape plan. The plan was altered now, she was in it. No way I could imagine leaving without her, even after this short period of knowing her. But I had to be patient. She wasn't ready.

46

After this beer fueled session I realized that meeting her was like hitting the proverbial jackpot. Could I be this lucky? Beside her looks, she was witty, a keen observer of people with a tongue like a razorblade, self-assured and direct. And above all she was genuine, a no bullshit girl. She expressed her opinions freely, sometimes rudely but always honestly.

The first few weeks we explored each other. For me it was like going on a treasure hunt, finding new pieces of gems at every turn. When you're in the daze and haze of love, everything your Goddess says or does is significant, revealing and wise. She finally exposes the truths you knew all along but were unable to express. She had a deep contempt for the toadying pseudo-communists worming their way up in life. Her father, a suppressed genius of a man, because he came from an old Hungarian noble family, was unable to find work worthy of his scientific talents.

"My Dad should be working in the Academy of Sciences. Instead he works in some engineering firm designing lathe machines. His boss couldn't lick his boots in the West. My father does all the work and he reaps all the benefits. But of course he is a good Party man. What a waste of talent. My father is a Renaissance man, he speaks three languages, can quote Goethe or Spinoza. Einstein was his classmate in Berlin before the Nazis; he is a champion skier, he used to play the organ before he was barred from the church. Now he is a depressed, bitter man. This is so fucking unfair! He taught me to see clearly through this dizzying totalitarian fuzz that surrounds us. I have no plans for the future anymore, I now I live for the day." Her outburst, her use of words greatly impressed me. She was too young for such insight.

As soon as I could, I arranged a trip to my uncle's villa by Lake Balaton. This took a little craftiness, since I was not allowed to take girls down there, the morals of my family being such. Clandestinely, my cousin and I had copies made of the keys to the place. I just had to be sure nobody planned a trip to the lake that weekend.

This was in early May, off season, so this wasn't a problem. Lily showed no signs of hesitation to come. She told her parents she was going to a friend's party at the other end of town and she would sleep over. Few people had telephones in those days, so she was in no danger of discovery. My hopes were up. Besides the doorway marathon kissing and necking sessions, I didn't, I couldn't make more advancement. And I loved her not only for her mind: her licentious body was a constant challenge to conquer. She looked prim, regal, detached to the outside world, but with me she showed her true colours. She was down to earth, not afraid to talk dirty, to delve into sex or anything else. This juxtaposition between the outside appearance and the inner truth gave her an even more, somewhat perverse appeal. She was a gem of a Gemini.

So we took the train to the lake. Lily's presence electrified the stuffy compartment the instant she stepped inside, the roving eyes of the male occupants settling on her constantly. Arriving to the lakeside, we proceeded to spend most of our money on booze, which was always freely available at railway stations (if not much else) and walked the half mile to the villa.

Fruit trees were in bloom, the buds on the branches straining under the pressure of the leaves about to be born. The sun shone unseasonably warm. The place was deserted, with that indescribable melancholy of summer places out of season. We checked ourselves into the Villa Vass. The musty smell of unopened rooms was chased out soon by the mellow breeze coming off the lake. We ate some lunch and proceeded to consume our supply of liquors.

We sat on the veranda, Lily's bare feet resting on my lap, and just talked. Mostly she talked and I eagerly listened. There was more to learn about her.

"Yes, I had boyfriends before. You think I saved my virginity, waiting for you to come on a white charger? But not one of them was worthy of me." She had this crystal laugh, like a twanging of an angel's harp.

"Am I worthy of you?"

"Time will tell. I am very popular, you know? I'm invited to parties all the time. Maybe I'll take you to one someday."

"It would be very generous of you, if I ever earn the honour."

We conversed and drank all afternoon on this most beautiful of days, watching the sun sliding leisurely across the lake of liquid gold, an occasional boat cutting a slowly healing wound on her body. To live through a day like this was worth being born.

How lucky I was to experience this euphoric high. Was it divine intervention that we met? Or a secret chemical signal we emitted, like bees, which drew us subconsciously together? There was nothing I cared for anymore: there was nothing significant in my life other than Lily. She was my world.

As dusk approached, I tried to orient Lily toward the bedroom. Holding her hand, leading us to the room, she halted at the door:

"Slow down, Peter. Just because I came with you here it doesn't automatically mean I'll go to bed with you at first opportunity."

"But this is a very rare opportunity, can't you see?"

"So you're an opportunist. You should join the Party. I'm not the kind of a girl who drops horizontal at the first chance. I hardly know you."

In my love-daze I resigned to this refusal, and later treasured this day all the more because of her admirable behaviour. She confessed later that she was tempted, but since she didn't really know me, her brain overruled her heart.

To be alone in an empty house was a rare opportunity indeed, since we had no other way to gain any privacy. We frequented her party circle, as she really was a popular beauty, in demand everywhere. At these parties we always drank a lot, sometimes going to work in the morning after an all-night shindig. Still woozy, generating irate looks from the dour, hapless masses crowding onto buses to go to work while we were laughing and kissing under the glorious halo of our bliss.

I was engrossed so much in this new feeling, I didn't see my mother much, neglected my friends and didn't care about my work. I just wanted to be with Lily all the time. She introduced me to her parents, a wonderfully warm, caring, easy-going couple, their only treasure being Lily. I behaved myself brilliantly, gaining their unworthy trust. After all I was the boy who eventually took their only child away from them, into the dangerous unknown, to the ambiguous Promised Land.

Finally, after months of looking for opportunities, one presented itself: a friend of Lily's threw a garden party in his parent's leafy hillside house; who naturally were away. It was a hot July night, the smog and noise of the city a memory below us. There was, as usual, a lot of drinking, mixing all the wrong combinations, just to get drunk quickly, as this was 'de rigeur'. We consumed our share diligently, and by about midnight we were spread out on the cool grass, looking at the stars, listening to the crickets.

Lily's head rested on my arm, her breathing felt under my other hand fondling her firm breast. We kissed with violent desire. My shaking hand unbuttoning her blouse met no resistance, neither my awkward hasty tugging of her skirt off. We were in a secluded corner of the garden, everybody too drunk to pay attention to us. I sensed Lily wanted me too, and so we made our first love under the stars, shaded by nodding sycamore trees, serenaded by love struck crickets, the faraway sounds of Van Morrison providing the background music. Of what I can remember, it was everything I dreamed of, and more. Lily was the Venus of my mythology. My fate was sealed there and then. I was hers.

Next day, recovered somewhat by noon, we took a tourist-boat cruise on the Danube. In my overhung, alcohol soaked high the world was a searingly beautiful place, the heart breaking splendour of the girl sitting across from me almost unbearably perfect and desirable. The old paddle wheeler puffed up and down on the river, sliding under the bridges to open up another panorama of palaces, churches, promenades, put there just for me to admire, to make the suitable prop for this day of glory. This was a floating dream I could never forget, the day too perfect to be true. I was the king of the world on that day, all the majesty of life mine, the luckiest man blessed with a woman of flawlessness.

So we immersed ourselves in the golden halo of our passion, searching for opportunities everywhere to fulfil our desire of each other. We were oblivious to the reality surrounding us. This was a spring of delirious love.

Our future was the one thing that threw a shadow over my happiness. I couldn't see any hope for us in my detested, loved, cursed country. I wanted out, to free myself by any means. This was the purpose of my life and even Lily's sudden thrust into it couldn't deter me. I wanted to be in the Land of Plenty, where young people lived in hippy communes, smoked marijuana, listened to Janis Joplin and Jimi Hendrix and still drove cars, lived in comfort, went to universities. With the scant information filtering through the Iron Curtain, I built a partly false image of this Dreamland. Now I had Lily, and I couldn't imagine my life without her. I had to convert her, convince her to come with me, leave her parents behind, risk being shot, start a new life in an alien land. But was she ready?

I *was* very ready to go. For months I'd been planning the escape, before I met Lily. I had the permit to go to Yugoslavia, with a guy, Tibi, whom I knew only through mutual friends. He was as keen as I was, and we figured it was better in a pair than going alone. We co-ordinated our vacation time. We had to leave in a few days. I wanted to know if I could convince Lily to come with me. If she would come, I would postpone the trip until she gets her papers and to hell with the rearing to go Tibi. I couldn't wait ay longer. I had to confront her. Time was not on my side.

We went for a dinner one night to our favourite hangout, a smoky old wine cellar in the Castle Hill. We were eating peasant grub, drinking wine from barrels by candlelight. After a few tumblers I breached the subject:

" Lily, are you happy living here ?" I asked.

"What do you mean?" She gave me an uncomprehending stare.

"I see no future for us here. Our jobs are meaningless, our wages are pitiful, we have no chance ever to have a place for ourselves. I could never be a scriptwriter here. Would I write for these liars? I'm tired of all the lies. I'm just sick of the lies. When I open a newspaper , I know they're lying, the reporter who wrote the article knows he is lying, the publisher knows they're lying, the newsagent who sells them knows the paper is full of lies. Everybody knows, and nobody dares to say 'Hey, the emperor has no clothes'.

My outburst threw her back. She furtively looked around, hoping nobody could hear my diatribe. There was a pause, she gulped her wine and stared into space, maybe for the first time looking into the future, seeing what it could hold for her

"What can you do about it?" she asked

"I have a plan. I've been planning this for a long time. We have to escape from Hungary. There is no other way. I tell you right now, I will try to escape, even if it will cost my life. I'm ready to go now, but if you come with me, I'll wait. I want to live in freedom, in the wealth of the West, have my own car, apartment, to eat good food. More than anything to be given a chance to write, to travel, and another thousand reasons to go. I love you more than you can imagine, so if we want to stay together, you have to come with me. I can't live in this place anymore."

There, I said it. I gave her an ultimatum. Her face was a picture of bewilderment. I wanted to give her my crazy plan in small dosages, but I had no time.

"Where to, when, how?" I could see she was biting, the idea taking a foothold in her brain behind those amber eyes. I told her about what I knew, how we could try to go through Yugoslavia and cross the border to Italy, as a friend has done it . He is living in America now, in his own apartment, drives a car, has a job etc.

"Aren't you always pining after all those wonderful clothes you see on Western tourists? Would you like to see all those exciting films you heard about but could never see here, listen to all the rock and roll you want, read forbidden books? "

"What about Mom and Dad? I'm all they have' she said.

"They could come out to visit us in a few years. They'll see how much better their daughters' life is. I'm leaving my mother behind too, and at least your parents have each other." I was callous about leaving my Mom behind, unthinking, putting the implications behind my feverish, focused, unwavering mind. I wanted out with the zeal of a fanatic. I would deal with the consequences later, I thought.

"What if we get shot?" she asked, looking into my eyes to detect a lie, while knocking back a tumblerful of wine.

"Not in Yugo. The worst can happen is they capture us and ship us back to Hungary."

The idea of leaving the country was new to her. It never crossed her mind to look into the future. She was 20 years old, couldn't blame her.

"I can't leave my parents, no way. They would die if something happened to me. I can't just decide on the spot if I want to do something like that? Let me think, please." She had another big gulp of wine and stared into space.

Seeing that I was dead set to go, she realized the only way to stay with me she had to come along or we would be torn apart. In my wine fuelled speech I described to her the wonders of the Other Side, kept emphasising the hopelessness of our future in Hungary.

I waited for her reply, but she just couldn't decide on such a short notice.

"Why can't we try to make it here? I'm not sure I want to abandon my life here, my parents, friends, the familiar. It's insane what you're planning to do. Let's just wait"

I threw her into deep water. It was obviously a sudden, shocking proposal.

It was a risky undertaking, and to be honest, I underplayed the dangers to her. I'd heard of guys who were captured by the Yugoslav border guards and shipped back, and were now sitting in jail.

I was in a terrible dilemma. I knew I could win her over, given time. Time I didn't have. My papers were good to go. A special permit was needed to travel to Yugoslavia, which was inserted into our internal passports, called Personal Identification Book. Every person had to carry it on him/herself. All the information in it had to be up to date: place of work, place of residence, marital status, military service, everything. This way the regime had total control over it's citizens. Just to get one of these inserts was a challenge: many applications and months of waiting for approval or rejection. If I didn't use mine who knew when I could get another one. I took my yearly two week vacation for this purpose. It was a choice of staying home with Lily or taking off to the West. I had dedicated the last five years of my life to getting out. I had to go.

One disturbing episode just before departure forced my hand further. The Personnel department of the factory summoned me one day. The dried out spinster , who was the dreaded dept. head invited me in and made me sit down in her office. Marx and Lenin gazed down from the walls. There was another person, a man I'd never seen before: a hard edged, handsome man in his forties. The red flag pin of the Communist Party decorated his lapel.

"This is comrade Kovacs, our party secretary. He wants to talk to you about your future here in our factory"

"Comrade Werner. We keep an eye on all our valued workers. You received the decoration of the Hero of Socialist Labour recently. You do good work for us. Don't you think it's about time you consider joining the Party? It is a rare privilege that we're offering a chance to apply for membership. It's time for you to be more politically active. Your fellow employees report that you visit rock and roll clubs, read western literature and are generally enthralled with the capitalist world. We think it's time for you to grow up and prove your true allegiance, to make a move toward the socialist way of life" At every sentence, he tapped his pen on the desk for emphasis.

This was the last thing I needed. My mind reeled: I worked for the award only because it came with a good sum of money. It looked like the fuckers had spies everywhere. I had to be more careful to whom and what I talked about. The silver lining was the travelling permit in my pocket, my possible escape hatch. I spouted the right answers of course:

"Until now I didn't think I was mature enough to join the party. It's an honour you invite me to apply. I will consider it and get back to you in two weeks. Is that satisfactory to you?" I turned my best eager face toward the rock solid man.

"No later. You have to come clean about your views and your willingness of commitment."

More tapping of the pen, then silence. It was a threat. But then I thought: if all goes well, Comrade Kovacs, I will enjoy the life of the rotten West and you'll have an idea of my commitment to your cause.

This happened a week before I left.

54

I still had this vague hope that Lily would follow me. How, with whom, when? I had   no answers to those questions. Thinking back now, I believe I wasn't completely sane at this juncture. I focused on the escape and nothing else mattered.

CHAPTER FIVE

I told my Mom I was going on a holiday to the Dalmatian Coast. To Lily I said nothing. With this cowardly act I think I shook her trust in me.

Tibi and I took the midnight train to Ljubljana, and from there another to the border city of Nova Gorica, which was divided in the middle.

The other side was Gorizia, in Italy. We arrived to the town in the morning. We had to waste a whole day. We didn't talk much. With the frightening unknown shadowing my every thought, Lily stayed on the hazy horizon. Somehow I pushed her image to the back of my mind. We ate little, gnawing on dry sandwiches we packed a day before, sitting on a park bench. Time just didn't want to move. The day was hot, a few lovers out for a stroll, bringing up painful flashbacks of Lily, Evening arrived when I thought it never will. We walked to the railway station. Here the border was demarcated by a chain link fence about six feet high topped with barbed wire. No watchtowers, just a simple fence. A patrol walked by every hour. We knew this from people who crossed here and wrote letters home. We tried to be inconspicuous as we could, we didn't wander about much, sat on a remote table in the waiting room.

When the time finally came, we bought tickets for a night train leaving at half past twelve to the nearest town. Sure enough a police patrol came to comb the waiting room, but we showed our tickets and they left us alone. After another interminable wait the train trundled in. We didn't get on, of course, but hid in some bushes by the station building. Once the train left, the place became deserted. The border fence was lighted up like a football stadium. The old fashioned stationmaster's office closed, the platforms empty. With gut wrenching anxiety we watched the fence across the train tracks. A mass of bent wire a few millimetres thick separated two worlds.

After about forty five minutes the border patrol came by, two guys, smoking, talking, strolling with casual boredom. They didn't even look in our direction. After waiting for ten minutes, seeing nobody around, I said: "Let's go." My heart was banging against its cage with such force I thought I could see my shirt moving. We dashed across the four pairs of rails, very conspicuous in the harsh lights, thinking the eye of the world was on us. We threw our bags across and mounted the fence with panicked haste, ignoring the barbs cutting into flesh. We were over in about a second, grabbed our bags and ran like Olympic sprinters. Nothing moved behind us, no shouting to stop, no sound. I mounted the rail ties by threes. These were Italian rails, Italian sleepers, Italian stones. I wanted to lay down and kiss them. The line veered away from the Yugoslav side and we soon came upon the Gorizia railway station.

This station was deserted too, except for the two policemen waiting for us. They must have been monitoring the border somehow. We climbed up to the platform, gasping for air. I could tell, they had seen this many times before. We let the two friendly men escort us to a waiting jeep. They drove us to the city police station. I wanted to see something of the wonderland, but all I could detect were dark leafy streets, parked cars. In the station they put us in an empty cell. They left the door ajar. It was a nice gesture. The fact that I was in the West didn't really sink in before I fell into an exhausted, haunted sleep.

Waking up in a police cell in a foreign country wasn't what I expected after my nightmarish dreams. After breakfast of toast and coffee we were driven back to the station and given two tickets to Trieste. Communication was by hand gestures.

I gaped at the wonderful scenery on the way. What I saw was the confirmation of my faith. In Trieste we presented ourselves at the station police along with the papers we were given in Gorizia. After some more intense Italian shouting and gesticulating, we were shepherded into another police jeep and driven up to Padriciano, the transit camp of multi storey concrete blocks. On the way there more proof of the lush, prosperous life presented itself to my hungry eyes. But I couldn't believe it, not really. It was a fantasy, something I will wake up from. My world was slipping away, I entered a netherworld. By the time we crossed the gates, I recovered somewhat; Tibi's presence from my old life confirmed that this was real.

At the camp we were fingerprinted, our documents taken away. We received some dubious looking pillows and a horse blanket and shown an iron bunk bed in a large room, full of fellow refugees. It had the sinister atmosphere of an army barrack. A few Hungarians gathered around us, asking about our escape and giving us the lowdown on camp life. Tibi quickly made buddies with them but I withdrew to my lower bed, laid down on the stained mattress and quietly descended into depths of anguish.

I made a terrible, terrible mistake. I left Lily behind. As all the happenings of the past two days came crashing down on to me, I had to answer the question: I did all this for what? To tear myself away from her for good? So I could never see her again? To shamefully escape, for not telling her anything, dropping out of her life like she didn't mean much to me?

This thoughtless dive into the unknown I just executed, landing me in this refugee camp was good for one thing; there was a certainty now: I couldn't live without my Lily. But could she follow me? How? I couldn't make it in this strange land, not without her.

I wanted to bang my head into the concrete walls of this desperate place I felt so stupid. Why didn't I wait, talk her into it, drag her with me if I must. We would make the perfect pair. The two of us could really conquer this new world, as I so shamelessly promised it to her.

The funny thing is, I should've been delirious. My lifelong ambition fulfilled. I was free, the opportunities were here. These guys were talking about going to America, Canada, Australia. The door was open, I just had to step through it. But if I went to these faraway countries I would never see her. She couldn't and wouldn't follow me. Would I ever meet anybody like her? Could I find somebody who could replace her? There was an unexplainable attraction between us down to the molecular level . There was nobody like her. What to do, what to do?

We received a dinner of tasteless pasta with oily lettuce in a big echoing hall. There were hundreds of us, all escapees from the clutches of communism. Most were upbeat, talking and laughing with release. I sat alone, my dour demeanour not inviting company. Tibi was already in the middle of a group of loud Hungarians, not paying attention to me.

I hurried back to our dorm and cuddled into my dirty warren, my mind churning and whirring. I was oblivious to the comings and goings of the room, immersed in my despondent world. After hours of grinding the wheels of my mind, I came to a decision: I will go back to Hungary and bring Lily out with me. A vague plan was forming in my overworked brain cells. It was extremely dangerous, a gamble. If I lose, I could end up in jail and never be able to leave the country. Looking back now, it was a reckless decision of a 25 year old who was desperately in love. Once I decided on the course of action, I relaxed and managed a few hours of sleep.

Next day we received our temporary camp ID cards cum meal tickets. We were free to go outside of the camp.

I had no documents, a few Yugoslav dinars and no idea how to do the escape in reverse. Nobody would be so insane to go back. But now I was just as determined and focused to go back as I was to coming out. I spent one more night in the camp. The next morning I managed to get a ride down to Trieste. I didn't have Italian lira to buy a ticket back to Gorizia, but I mounted the first train nevertheless. I dodged the conductor, changing cars at every station, locking myself in to the toilet at one time.

I made it back to this leafy, restful little town, where life moved slow and easy. I couldn't risk the vaulting of the fence in reverse. I had to go outside and skirt the city until I stumbled back into the iron embrace of the Wrong Side. I hung around the park in the middle of the town. I was very hungry. I had hours to contemplate my dire situation, judging the merits of staying against the madness of going back. But my longing for Lily overrode any other arguments. Not going back was not an option.

Evening finally came. I strolled slowly toward which looked like the outskirts of town. I had a hunch which way was Yugoslavia. I entered a grove of some trees, the city lights diminishing behind me. I made some noise, stepping on branches, stumbling on a root. There was no sign of any kind of demarcation line. I kept going toward a group of bright lights, which I assumed to be a border crossing. I thought I could just go around it. The forest turned denser, the going harder. Then from the dark belly of the trees came a sharp shout:

"Stoy!" Stop.

I stopped, along with my heart. A blinding torchlight in my eyes followed. I couldn't see beyond the light, but I heard a familiar click-clock of an AK 47 being armed.

"Davay" Go. I knew this much of the Slavic languages. I turned around and with the light on my back and a gun barrel between shoulder blades, we moved on. From the two words I heard I could just make out of a voice of a young, equally scared man. He had the gun on my back, so he shouldn't be as frightened as I was, I thought.

This is it, I said to myself. I stumbled at the first hurdle, my hopelessly unrealistic return thwarted at the very beginning. Maybe Lily will visit me in jail, I mused with bitter irony.

He guided me onto a sort of trail, and after a few minutes we entered a guardhouse. Here was light, and I could make out two pimply faced youngsters. First, one of them asked: "nationalny?" " Vengry" I answered , my country's name in the Slavic languages. After some intense talk, one picked up a phone and called someone. They motioned to me to sit down on a chair and we waited. I wished I could talk to them, they were just kids:

"Come on, boys, we're just a couple of guys who love Rock and Roll, drinking, girls, dancing, we're the same. Under your uniforms you are same as me. Forget about all this bullshit with borders and patrols and guns. It's all adult stuff. Let me go. I'm no criminal, never harmed anybody, just a lad who want to go back to his love."

We just eyed at each other, waited. Nobody talked. After about half an hour a jeep pulled up and a man who looked like an officer stepped inside the hut. He was in his forties, with the bearing of a professional soldier. The boys snapped to attention and one of them reported. To my surprise, the officer addressed me in broken Hungarian. He must have been ethnic Hungarian, since one time this area of the country was part of the Austro-Hungarian Empire.

His questions came in fast succession: where are my papers, what was I doing at the border, which way was I going, did I want to go to Italy?

I was ready with my story. Whether it was believable or not was another question, but it was the best I could make up: I was on holiday, on a beach in Opatija,(Abbazia) swimming in the sea. I left my belongings in the care of a nice young couple. When I came back after a big swim, the nice couple disappeared and so did my wallet and ID book. I hid some money in my shoe just for back-up and now I just wanted to go back home. I bought tickets to Nova Gorica and I wanted to see how Italy looks like from a distance before I go home.

This was a pretty shaky story, but how else I could explain my wanderings around the border. I could never reveal I came back from Italy. The truth wouldn't be believable to anybody.

He escorted me to the jeep and we drove to some barracks on the edge of town. He came to a halt in to the deserted courtyard. A soldier appeared and the two of them escorted me to an empty cell.

"I'll interrogate you in the morning" he promised, banged the door shut and left me to my demons. The closet sized room had a wooden cot and a bucket in the corner, illuminated by a 40 watt bulb. No sounds penetrated the walls. I laid down on the filthy bed and staring at the ceiling I slowly disseminated how I casually destroyed my life with my blind love and stupidity. I was very hungry. Only the Italian camp breakfast sat deep in my bowels like a reminder of another, thrown way life. I fell asleep, the needs of the body overriding any other matters.

At dawn a surly border guard tossed a bucket of water and a rag in, and indicated for me to wash the floor. Half asleep, hardly comprehending my desperate standing in the world, I dutifully washed the grimy floor, rinsed, washed again. It gave me something to do: a type of work therapy. Soon after, the same uniform gave me a slice of bread and a hunk of industrial grade marmalade. I almost chocked on it I was so hungry. He came back later and escorted me to the officer from the night before.

He asked all the questions again and more, all about my background, my workplace, residence etc. This time he wrote everything down on sheets of paper. He kept looking at me with probing eyes, taking the measure of me. Once he finished his interrogation, he took out a typewriter from a drawer and started to knock away, looking into his hand writing. This is his report to the police, or to the courts, I thought. A dark, despondent shroud descended on my very being. The worst was that I could only blame myself for the failure I was, the fiasco I had gotten myself entangled in.

"I don't believe in your story to start with" said the man, looking up after he finished his typing,

"I'm sure you've tried to cross into Italy. We've seen your kind around here before. Maybe you had your ID stolen, maybe you threw it away. I don't know. You better go back to your country. I never ever want to see you here again. If we catch you again we'll throw you in jail for good and send you back in as somebody who tried an illegal border crossing. You understand my Hungarian, don't you?" I nodded enthusiastically.

"I tell you what I'll do. I'll send you to the bus station, and you'll buy tickets to Ljubljana and then to Budapest. Thank your lucky stars or God or whoever, to meet me. Now get out of my sight."

I walked out of the office still not believing my luck. The guy let me go! My life's not over yet! Another guard, a private looking one drove me to the bus station and waited behind me in the line-up until I bought my tickets to Hungary. My money was good only 'til the first town inside the country, but it was Hungary and it was good enough for the border guard.

I had my rucksack and nothing else to keep me company. I knew my ordeal wasn't over. The riskiest part still lay ahead of me. Maybe my luck would hold out. My guardian angel had some work cut out for her and I hoped she was up to the task.

The bus ride to Ljubljana was uneventful. The next bus to Hungary didn't leave until evening. I'd spent all my money on the bus fare, and was again starving. There was nothing I could do about it. I wasted some more time loitering in the city. Fear really started to get hold of me. I was going behind the Iron Curtain. I knew what it was like, I knew very well. But there was no way to back off now. I had to face whatever happened. Lily or bust.

The bus rumbled through the night, packed with Hungarians returning from seaside holidays. Dread tightened my insides with ever increasing ferocity as we counted down the kilometres. At dawn we reached the border. A sleepy guard in the familiar uniform came on, asking for everybody's ID. I sat in the back. The man inevitably closed in on me. It was fate approaching with a Kalashnikov slung across his shoulder. When I answered negative for his perfunctory call for my ID, an alertness came over his features.

"You step down and come to the office." The familiar attitude. As I walked the long aisle of the bus following the soldier, the passengers watched me like someone walking the plank.

In a smoky, bright room I sat down in front of a fat, mean looking captain. A funeral pyre of cigarette butts in an ashtray and a cup of coffee with a metallic glint decorated his desk.

"What do you mean they stole your ID? Did you report it to the local police?

"No, comrade captain. I didn't know I had to. I don't speak the language. It was only my fourth day of my holiday, but I turned back right away. I don't have any money left. I want to go home. I have a responsible job, I am a factory supervisor and a candidate member of the party."

I maybe overdid it with my Party shtick, but the earnest, indignant face I made had an impact. Obviously the man didn't know what to do. It was Sunday, all offices closed. To him, with the border incident left out of course, the story sounded believable. Most people wanted to get out of Hungary, not to get back in.

He took all my information down, every detail he could come up with. I had all the answers down pat. In the meantime the bus was idling in the parking lot, sleepy and indignant passengers inhaling their cigarettes outside.

"First thing you do tomorrow morning is you report the theft to your district police office and ask for them to issue to you a new one. Do we understand each other?" he asked.

"Of course, comrade captain."

I got on the bus, the fellow passengers grumbling hostile comments, but I couldn't care less. I was on my way to Lily's arms. If she will forgive me, that is. I wasn't thrown off at the station where my ticket was good for. I stayed on 'til Budapest.

I arrived on a hot summer afternoon to the city I wanted to escape from so much. Nothing changed, nobody paid attention to me. I was the only one who knew: I'd been on the other side. I'd seen it, I knew how it was. It was nice, unimaginably nicer than what we have here. I would go back, but with my love this time.

My first act was to find a phone booth to call her.

"Hi Lily, it's Peter." My heart was in my throat, my voice shaky.

"Peter, where are you calling from?" A pause.

"Are you in Italy?" More pause." Why are you calling me? You left me without saying a word. We're finished."

She hung up. I dialled again, but it was busy, as I expected. I was dizzy; from hunger, from sleeplessness, from the realization that maybe I risked everything for naught.

I tried to call her a few more times. I had no other option, but to go to her place.

The so familiar ride on the streetcar to her apartment had a strange-ness about it. I was somebody else holding onto the leather straps, swaying with the rolling tram. The new me saw things differently, a returning astronaut from another planet.

Lily opened the door, I guess half expecting me. A symphony of emotions flooded my tired brain: the joy of seeing her, the burning shame of deserting her, the fear of losing her, I couldn't say a word. My legs almost gave out. She was even more beautiful than I imagined. She had make-up on, dressed nicely.

"What are you doing here?" Her voice was harsh, uncompromising.

"I had to see you. Can I come in? I'll explain everything."

"There is no way you can explain away what you did. We're finished. Didn't you hear me on the phone? Leave before my parents come out."

"I won't leave until you hear me out. Just give me a chance to tell you what happened to me. I came back for you from Italy."

She hesitated for a second, but then relented.

"Come straight to my room. My parents don't want to see your face again."

The wonderfully familiar, tiny converted old servant's room greeted me as a returning prodigal son. There was room only for a cot and a chair. She sat on the bed, an expectant look on her face.

"Do you have anything to eat? I haven't eaten for forty eight hours."

It looked like this touched a chord in her. She came back from the kitchen with a bowl of leftover goulash soup, cold. She wanted to warm it up, but I couldn't wait. I disgustingly slurped the soup down, eating loaf after loaf of bread with it. She didn't say a word, my loud eating noises the only sound.

Once I finished, I could start my story.

"You have to understand: people can make mistakes. I got blinded by my mad desire to get out of this place. I've worked toward this goal since I was a teenager. I could see no other opportunities to escape. You know I've tried to convince you to come with me. I was in Italy, inside the refugee camp. I could have gone to any country, but I came back for you after I realized I can't live without you. I want to go again, but with you."

She looked at me, maybe a foot away, pain shading her eyes I loved so much.

"Just tell me, how could you do this? How could you leave me without saying a word? 'Together Forever' that was our corny motto wasn't it? Even though it was so cheesy, I believed it. You broke my heart. It's a cliché, but I can't express it any better. I thought I'll never see you again. You can't really love me if you could do this. You said you came back for me. Why should I believe you now? Were you in Italy at all?"

I took out a plastic pouch from my rucksack. International Red Cross was stencilled in bold letters on the outside. I opened it: inside a Gillette shaving foam and blade, a Mennen after shave, a Colgate toothpaste, Lavoris mouthwash. This was the content of the toiletries case they gave me in the camp. It was full of western products unavailable in our country. She glared at it, then handled the pieces like an archaeological find.

"You're truly insane. What would have happened if they searched your bag? How would you explain this? You are the luckiest guy on Earth to pull this off. You're the bravest or stupidest of all people."

I knew I impressed her with my boldness, there was hope now.

"Now you know. I had to prove to you that I really came back for you from There. I risked everything. I, the romantic fool, thought it would still be better to see you on visiting days in a jail than not seeing you ever. How is that for crazy love? We'll go back there together. I know the way now. You'll be risking less." But I didn't make an impact:

"I am going out shortly. To a date."

"To a date? With whom? "

"You don't know the guy. He is an engineering student. He is not planning to leave me without a word. He's crazy about me. He lives on the hill in a nice house with his parents."

If she wanted me to be jealous, she succeeded.

"This was fast. Was he kept in reserve, just in case I bolt? How long have you known this guy?"

"Peter, you have no right to question me like this. Our affair was over and I found the best way to get over my pain and humiliation was to see others. After I cried through two nights, my Mom advised me to

go out and find other young men, better ones than the one I cried my eyes out for. No man worth it, darling, no man. That's what she said."
"
"Did you do anything with him?" I asked, fearing the answer.

"Even if I liked the guy, I'm not that easy, you know that. You were gone for less than a week"

"Please Lily, don't leave. I had to go all the way to an Italian refugee camp to realize how much I love you. Like I said, I can't imagine my life without you. Let's go out, you and me somewhere tonight. Phone your university student. Tell him the love of your life, risking jail or worse, just returned and you want to live the rest of your life with him. Well, I don't really mean to tell him like this. Actually, don't even bother to phone him." I knew I sounded pathetic, grovelling like this. But I was desperate.

"There is no way I will put myself through this again. I can't just forget what you did to me. There is no redemption for you. Better go home. Your Mom thinks you're holidaying in Croatia. I don't think I want to see you again. I think we really had something special but you fucked it all up."

I was speechless. I failed. I did all this insanely dangerous return for nothing. I could be waiting for a transfer to America in the camp. Now I was back in the place I dreamed of escaping, for years. This was beyond devastating.
There was silence for a while between us, just the dense cloud of thoughts swirling around our heads. Finally she spoke again:

"You should have thought about consequences. But enough of this talk. Please go."

And with that, she rose and escorted me to the door. She opened it and I walked out. I wanted a last look, but she turned her head away, maybe to hide a tear, and closed the door. I stood in that doorway for a long time. The word devastation doesn't give justice for what I felt. The world was black and white, or rather grey, void of life affirming colour.

Finally I descended the stairs, past the doorway of so many memories, onto the street and traffic and people. I boarded the streetcar

68

home. I couldn't avoid remembering my euphoric night ride that seemed so long time ago, in a different life.

I rang the doorbell and my mother opened it.

"Peti! Oh my God, Jesus, Mary and Joseph! You're back so early. What happened?"

She almost fainted in her relief and joy to see me.

"I came back earlier because I got robbed on the beach." When her questions started to come, I continued to lie blatantly. About my stolen papers, money, the journey back to her. My dear, trusting, loving mother believed me as any mother wants to believe her deceitful son.

I still had a week holiday left. One last risky act was left to complete my trail of deception. On Monday morning I repaired to the familiarly menacing district police office. Now my story changed again. I was in a big outdoor dance club on Margaret Island on Saturday night. I got drunk and danced all night. Somehow the Personal Identification book fell out of my pocket. I only discovered it on Sunday morning.

The sparrow faced maiden behind the small window took my name and advised to wait a week. Somebody was bound to find it and turn it in. It was no use for anybody else- she advised. Come back by Friday.

Not surprisingly nobody turned the booklet in. I gathered all the necessary documents and applied for a new ID and within a few weeks I was a relieved owner of one. I thought all my nefarious doings of the past were erased and I could start my quest to escape anew. But it wasn't that simple as it turned out.

The long lonely week of leftover holiday didn't want to end. I had nothing to do but bury myself in my self-loathing, grinding my mind to a pulp. Nothing seemed to matter now with my life without Lily. I got drunk most nights in the neighbourhood "drinking shop" (yes that was the un-poetic but realistic name of the cheap watering holes). I told my mother I broke up with Lily, and she saw my drinking as my way of dealing with it.

Monday morning came as a relief of sorts, starting to work. But on the first day I had an accident: in a lab I was pouring vitriol, which is a 100% concentrated sulphuric acid into a high funnel when my hand slipped and the liquid run down my arm. It was like someone burned my skin with a blowtorch. I ran screaming to the water tap, fellow workers rushing to my aid. My skin was peeling off in red sheets. They rushed me to a hospital for burns. After various treatments with ointments, I was put to bed. I was lying there, my arm pulsating with pain, but somehow I felt this was a good thing. It took my mind off Lily, my stupidity to return. I could concentrate on this sensation. Some pills I took put me to a dreamless sleep.

My mother came next morning, all worried, bringing food and goodies with her. I was to stay in the hospital for a week. There were horribly burned patients on this ward, so I counted myself lucky. I couldn't hold a book up, so I didn't have much to do but think.

It was on the first day, evening time, after a dreadful dinner that a miracle happened. In the bright outline of the door a vision appeared, an angel descending in a halo of light. She looked around hesitantly, clearly horrified by the scene when she spotted me. She carried a bunch of flowers and a bottle of schnapps. My heart almost jumped out of my chest. This vision was my beautiful Lily. I was afraid it was only a dream. She sat down to the chair next to me. Her fragrance overwhelmed the grisly hospital smell. I couldn't say a word. She finally spoke:

"What happened to you?" There was concern in those eyes. I found my voice:

"I burned myself, stupidly. But that's a minor matter. How come you're here? Is it a charity visit?"

"Your Mom phoned, begging me to see you. She is very worried about your state. I didn't mind to come though. I was very determined to leave you out of my life, as I swore I would. But when I saw your bastard face in that doorway, gaunt, unshaven, hungry, to tell you the truth, I was delighted. Maybe I hid it well, and I tried to stick to my decision. The last week was tough. I almost went to your place. I was waiting for a sign from you but it didn't come. So when your Mom phoned, I rushed here. So how is your arm? You'll be able to use it again?"

"I'll be dancing with you in no time if you're able to forgive me. We have one more visiting hour to ourselves. Thanks for the flowers and let's open that booze and talk."

This we did. We had a shot from plastic tumblers, giving us a needed lift. In hushed tones I told her about my new ID book on the way, how lucky I was that I got away with my deception.

"Lily, listen to me" I whispered. "We have to get away, that's the only way for our life together. I've seen some of it. You'll be happy there. We have to get married. I can't get down on my knees, I don't have a ring. This is so unromantic, but it can't wait. Would you marry me? We are together again, it's real. Time to start planning our future. This is something I always wanted to do; marry you and get the hell out of here."

"I had a lot of time to think last week. I can see your point. The fact is that you came back for me proves your love. You're right, we have no future here. I'm ready to go with you. It's a jump to the unknown for me but I'm ready to take that chance.

"It's not unknown. I know the way now, it'll make it less risky. We'll conquer the world Lily, you and me"

Big words, fuelled by drink, but I felt an awesome sense of relief, of liberation. Our destiny was to be together. I didn't feel pain in my arm, the grim hospital room was a beautiful place, my princess was sitting by my side. It was fantastic to be alive.

CHAPTER SIX

She visited me every night after work that week. My arm was healing nicely and her heart was healing too. Since I could get out of bed, we found a grotty little alcove in the old building, complete with two chairs, away from eager ears. This time I talked. Now that she agreed to escape, I dazzled her with the little I saw of the West in the three days I was there. The shops bulging with everything we were pining for here; the fabulous foods spilling onto the sidewalks, the shiny sport cars, the cleanliness, orderliness, the kindness of the people, even those in authority.

"Remember the movie 'Easy Rider'? Imagine driving through America in a big car, cruising on the endless highways, the spectacular panorama of the West unfolding under the limitless sky, the freedom of it all? Strolling on Via Veneto like Mastroianni did in Dolce Vita? Taking in Carnaby Street in London among the hippies, maybe spotting Mick Jagger? Or listening to Jimmy Hendrix in San Francisco with the flower people? It could all be possible."

"You're a dreamer, but a persuasive one. I wish it could come true."

"It will if we do it. I am certain we'll succeed"

I could see I infected her. This was our sole subject of discussion during that glorious week in that wretched hospital. She kept smuggling booze in, cheap sweet dessert wines which we gulped down from the bottle. We even managed a few necking sessions, away from seeing eyes. The more I fell back into my old Lily-craze, the more I realized how lucky I was to recover this treasure which I so callously threw away. That she took me back was all the proof of her love I needed. Every night, after she left, I lay in my bed, staring at the ceiling in a tipsy euphoria, seeing her face behind my eyelids, drifting off to dreamy sleep.

During these long boozy talks, we eventually moved from "theoretical discussions" to actual planning. I explained everything to her again, to make it sink in this time.

"Listen now and listen well. The only Western border with Hungary is Austria, and as you know, it's impenetrable. We are inside a giant prison. Even to go near to the border area you needed a special permit, and you had better have a damn good reason to go there."

"I know all that. Talk about how to get out" my inpatient darling interjected.

"That's why we go through Yugoslavia. Now I'll be your guide. That borders is not impossible to cross, as I proved it to you personally. To be honest, it will be more difficult than with Tibi since we have find another way to cross over. We both had to apply for that special permit, me for the second time. Are you with me, fully committed?"

"Do I have a choice? Yes. I want to get going, get married and get the hell out of this place."

For another two week I convalesced at home, pulling in full pay. We met every night, sitting in little "espresso" coffee bars, conspiring.

"Once we settled in America and have a passport and some money, the next thing I want us to do is travel. There is an awesome world out there. I have been reading about places you wouldn't know existed. Do you know there are still head hunters in Borneo? There is a railway line in Australia through the Nullarbor Plain which runs in a straight line for four hundred kilometers. Do you know that the water swirls in a different direction in a sink down under? There is a plain in Burma called Bagan, dotted with over two thousand Buddhist temples, as far as the eye can see. In India, on the shores of the Ganges River they burn bodies and throw the ashes in the water. And downriver people bathing in it. I want to see all these places and more: the carnival in Rio, the pyramids of Egypt and so on; the list endless. Would you come with me?

"Do I have a choice now, after what you put me through? Of course I'll go with you. Just God help us"

Before the wedding, we had to have a place to live, if only temporarily. To find a sublet for a few months was a challenge. There was a dreadful housing shortage along with all the other shortages. People spent all their life co-habiting in apartments, two or more families, from babies to grandparents sharing one kitchen, one bathroom. The possibilities for conflict were endless. A sublet was a step down from there, even more degrading. Through Lily's Mom's contacts, we secured a little basement "room", more like a cell, iron bars on the high window, showing the legs of passers-by. Exposed pipes run overhead. We had a privilege to know if someone had a dump upstairs by the torrent of cascading water. The plaster was peeling form the walls, bathroom was in the wood storage area frequented by rats. And it was expensive. But, hey, did we care? It was for a few months, until we bolt. And there was space for a bed, which made it all acceptable. A bookshelf and a table completed the "décor". We bought a second hand B&W TV, watching fuzzy images on one channel. We stuck up cut-outs from smuggled-in western magazines, the pictures of cars, boats, food, shampoos and cosmetics, all that glorious bourgeois decadence we pined for. These were the icons we worshipped on the stained walls of our little hole, the pictorial proof of a better life we were aiming for, ready to risk our lives to get there.

But first the business of matrimony had to be taken care of. Looking back now a few decades later, I can see what a pitiful little celebration it was.
Not that we cared much. A fancy wedding won't make a good marriage, Lily wisely stated. The paper proving our matrimony was all we wanted.

Our wedding was a low key affair. The ceremony took place in one of the state "wedding halls", in lieu of the church. The place was a cross between a ballroom and a bordello: chandeliers, velour wallpaper, chintz and brocade. Outside was a line waiting to get married.. We had fifteen minutes.

The wedding march was piped in and it was our turn. Lily and I walked in, holding hands to a drape covered table where a woman of officious bearing awaited us. She had the sash of the Hungarian tricolour across her considerable chest. She made a short speech: it could have been a tape recorded one for it's spontaneity. We exchanged rings, signed papers and we were husband and wife. Not a wedding a girl would dream about. I asked Lily about it later:

"I'm not a 'dreaming of a white wedding -kinda girl. We got the papers, we could live together, and most important we could get the hell out of this place together. Big fancy weddings are for pretentious assholes."

Our parents, a group of friends, colleagues gathered on this hot spring day at this wedding hall to wish us good luck. We needed it. Lily wore a pale blue suit custom made for the occasion. Years later in Canada, finding it among our reject clothes, we wondered how the ill-fitting, poor quality garment was considered a fine wedding dress then.

My mother was not thrilled by my marriage to Lily. She called her a "dangerous woman", the one who would steal her only son away from her. Little did she know, it was *me* who stole her from her parents. And she was also an only child. I was so blinded by love then, all I cared about was to be with Lily, take her with me to the Other Side and live my life with her 'til I died.

Afterward we had a small reception at Lily's parents' apartment, and by late evening we were on our way to Lake Balaton, to a "honeymoon" in the family villa. This time we were there legitimately, the hypocrisy of it never registering to our family.

After two weeks of a feverish love-in by the lake, we moved into our new lodgings.

We applied for the permit to travel to Yugoslavia right away on the pretext of a honeymoon, but we were rejected. I had to do something about Comrade Kovacs's threat. I went to see him in his own, opulent office. I confessed to the errors of my ways, and promised I would devote my free time to study the classics (read Marx, Engels, Lenin) so in time, maybe in a year I would have enough class consciousness to apply. Right now I was just not ready. He being such doctrinaire, brainwashed specimen, by spouting the right slogans I made him believe in my sincerity.

I never talked about my private life again to anybody in the workplace, but made sure I dropped hints of my interest of the works of Lenin and Co. I could see no other way to dodge the bullet. I was hoping this way the permit would come through easier. I worked diligently, giving the impression of a party-worthy young man. Lily was a member of the KISZ, the Communist Youth, so that was a good point in her application.

This rejection set us back, something we hadn't anticipated. We had to endure a whole year in that claustrophobic basement room. We lived in a suspended space, hovering in between our old life and the new one we envisioned for ourselves.

Living for one year in close quarters let me know the real Lily. She had faults. It was a surprise after my honeymoon-ish euphoria has settled down. First of all, being an only child, she was a spoiled princess. Cooking, doing laundry (by hand washing, what else was there?), cleaning, all were alien concepts to her. We ate mostly in our institute canteens, bland greasy fodders during daytime. There wasn't even a appliance where she could learn to cook.(If she wanted to). These were the sixties in Hungary, men didn't do domestic chores, and since she was an early liberated woman, we didn't do housekeeping.

She was also a very impatient person. She hated waiting for anything, especially to get out of our little cave. She liked to be served, and slowly she broke me into a devoted husband who catered to her every whim. She was vain, a quality I found engaging in a woman, especially somebody as pretty as she was. She liked to drink, sometimes reaching an aggressive stage. She was also the jealous type. To compensate for her lack of domestic skills, she was a master of the cosmetic arts, hairstyling and other, more important skills! Her tongue was as sharp as ever, and she wouldn't take shit from anybody, including me. This was all fine by me. I loved her, faults and all. And she was no wallflower when she had a chance to point out any of my shortcomings. This was married life, get used to it, I told myself.

John Lennon said "Love is all you need" I kept reminding myself.

Other than each other, nothing was of significance in our life there.

We didn't pay much attention to friends, work, happenings. The present in Hungary was already our instant past, something we knew would leave behind.

We got our permit after a second try, on a Tuesday in June, and planned to leave on the following Saturday. This was cause for celebration. One last time we repaired to our Castle Hill dungeon, and with the papers in our pockets, we fell into drunken, feverish talk. The fear of the unknown, the most debilitating fear, was behind me. I had confidence, and by now Lily placed her trust in me. We talked in whispers. I knocked a candle over, spilling molten wax onto her dress, tipping a tumbler of wine onto the rough wooden table; I was in ecstasy. I thought the road to freedom was open.

But two days later, upon my arrival home from work, our landlady delivered a devastating news:

"Peter, a telegram came for you. I think it's from the Ministry of Defence. I signed for it."

I almost fainted. I tore open the paper, and there it was:

"The Commander of the Hungarian Peoples' Army orders you, Peter Werner (my name was typed in at the blank space) to report on July 16th 1970 at 08:00 to the Szolnok Infantry Barracks for reserve officer training for a duration of six months. Detailed instructions to follow."

My mind was reeling. This couldn't be true. Not now, not in the last minute, not after all the tribulations, all the dangers, heartaches, We betted our lives on this. Six months later would be winter, therefore another year wasted in our claustrophobic dungeon, putting our life on hold for another useless twelve months. My landlady sensed my agony and asked:

"What is this for Peter. Something's wrong? You look pale."

"It's just a note to report for some reserve duty. Nothing serious. Thank you for signing for it".

I tore into our room. Lily wasn't home yet. I threw myself on the bed, staring the peeling paint on the ceiling. My panic slowly subsided and was able to think. There was only one way out of this. We had to leave that night. We had the papers and I knew there was a midnight train leaving for Yugoslavia every day. We had to be on it. I was blind to the danger of being charged with desertion, a very serious martial crime in communist Hungary. I would risk everything on this one shot.

When Lily walked in, seeing me on the bed fully clothed, then seeing my face, she knew something terrible happened. I showed her the telegram without a word. She blanched.

"Looks like God doesn't want us to go, to abandon our parents" she said with resignation, the collapse of our hopes darkening her face.

"No, no, NO! We go tonight. This is the only chance we have. Start packing a few things. The train leaves at midnight. We have the papers. There is no way in the world I go back to the Army, to waste another year. And our permits will expire by then. How do you know we'll get another pair next year?" I was almost foaming at the mouth, a racehorse at the starting gate. My fever was infectious. Lily quickly warmed to the idea.

"Yes, let's go for it. I can't live in this shithole for another year. And who knows if we would get this chance again. I have to tell my parents though. I must."

After some more panicked discussion, we packed hastily and walked over to her parents' apartment. They knew we wanted to escape, but the sudden, unexpected leave still shook them up. We had a heartbreakingly solemn dinner with them. They looked like they were in shock.

We could never forget the two lonely, bent figures waving goodbye on the street, their sorrowful faces forever etched in our memory. Tears cascaded down on Lily's face as she stared through the rear window of the taxi until they disappeared around the corner.

As far as they knew, we could be heading to our death, or to a long jail sentence; into the frightening unknown. My insane determination infected Lily by now, and she was as ready to risk it all as I was.

We never told my mother we were leaving. I'm ashamed to admit, I didn't trust her enough. What if she, in her desperation to hold onto me, reported us to the police? If I told her we were going back to Yugo, she would know why. We would never have a chance to escape again. I just couldn't risk it. In her subsequent letters she told me how much I hurt her by this act,

We bought our tickets at the train station, changed some money at a 24hr booth, but it was still a half hour before departure time. At every booming of the loudspeaker I expected to hear my name, calling me to report to the station's military post, or a patrol to walk into our compartment to arrest me. When the train started with a sudden jerk, I was relieved somewhat. But we still had to cross the border to Yugoslavia.

We tried to sleep for the few hours until the train stopped. We waited and waited in the early morning dawn. Finally two border guards entered, not bothering to knock. We were the last to be examined. One of the guards was holding a clipboard with typewritten pages on it. Holding my permit in his hand, he scanned the many names on the pages. Sweat trickled down on my spine, my eyes fixed on the velvet headrest.

"What's your purpose to visit Yugoslavia?

"We are on a honeymoon, Comrade Officer" I said with a hint of bashfulness.

He took an appreciating look at Lily, stamped our papers and left without a word. The train still wouldn't move. I looked outside at the deserted station, willing the engine to start pulling the wagons behind it. Lily and I didn't talk, just gazed into each other's eyes with desperation and hope.

We arrived in the morning to Ljubljana, sleepy, and hungry. There was no train connection this time. We had a whole day to waste. The bus to Nova Gorica wasn't leaving until five in the afternoon. The waiting, the aimless loitering was more difficult to deal with than the danger we would face later. We had no desire to eat despite our empty stomachs, the nervous tension wracking our tired bodies. Finally departure time came.

An hour into our journey a border guard got on the bus and stood right by our seat. We were convinced: this was it: we would be taken off at the next stop and deported back to Hungary. The fear and tension turned my guts to liquid. At the next town I dashed to the toilet, but upon returning, the guard was still there, standing by our seat unmoved.

We arrived close to midnight. The guard got off and never even looked at us. Just returning to his garrison I guess. But our paranoid minds played a cruel trick on us. We were right where we wanted to be. Gorizia and Italy beckoned. I knew we couldn't do the border fence-jumping with Lily. We had to go around the city until we hopefully stumble onto Italian territory.

Lily suggested a double shot of slivovica at the bus station, to give us some Dutch-courage. We needed it. Our beacon of hope was an illuminated bastion in the distance, which I knew was in Italy.

With two stuffed handbags, we nonchalantly strolled in the deserted streets, heading to the outskirts of town, when our hearts skipped a beat. Around a corner, under harsh streetlights, blocking our way, a couple of motorcycle police were standing, talking. In a desperate, hopeless act I grabbed Lily, and started to kiss and hug her, trying to give the impression of ambling lovers out for a stroll. I was afraid to look toward the cops, we just held onto each other in a mock lover's embrace while ice formed around my heart. We heard the two guys talking in Slovenian, smelled their biting tobacco, but just kept strolling, the big bags advertising our intentions. After a block, we inhaled and kept on going.

Once out in the countryside, we quickly lost our way. We choose a moonless week on purpose, so it was too dark to see anything. Finally I spotted an outline of a house and a glint of chrome on a car.

"I'll check out the licence in that car, see if it's Italian" I said to my brave, exhausted, determined love. As I strolled ever slowly toward the car, a dog started to bark and a light came on, so I retreated in a hurry. Some more aimless wandering later, we found a gravel track. I advanced slowly not knowing where the trail lead, when with a painful bang, I kicked some metal plate strung across the road, sending a booming, bell like sound across the valley. Now we were sure we would be caught, but after some terror-filled minutes, nothing happened. Somehow through some bushes we spotted the lighted tower, so now we knew which way to go. Except a seemingly impenetrable thorn bush blocked our way. We couldn't find a way around it and in desperation, I told Lily, we would have to try tomorrow somewhere else. But my stout hearted Amazon, fuelled by the slivovica, said:

"If I came this far, I'm not going back. We just have to break through this thorn bush from hell" And that we did. Later in the refugee camp the local medic was extracting spikes from our flesh for weeks. Our clothes were shredded in seconds. Lily came in a mini skirt, so not to arouse suspicion, the red rivulets running down her alabaster tights and calf were like the claw marks of a giant cat.

In absolute exhaustion, bathing in our own sweat, after stumbling across ploughed fields, we spotted a lamp post. Leaving Lily behind, I cautiously approached the brightly lit spot. On the post was a sign in Italian. I can't describe the feeling that came over me. It was almost better than orgasm, an euphoric, heart lifting, dizzying high, nothing I felt when I crossed with Tibi. This was final. Somehow, on a subconscious level I never totally felt my escape was for real at that time.

"We are in Italy," I yelled as I ran back to her. We sat in the freshly turned earth in the middle of the night, and cried. With my torrent of tears I released twenty seven years of bottled up resentment, fear, inhumanity. It was coming up for air after an agonizingly long time underwater. Now I could stay here, my Lily right beside me. I've beaten impossible odds. It was all worth it.

We threw away our shredded, sweat and blood-soaked clothes and changed into some new ones. I wondered ever after what that Italian peasant made out of finding some bloody, torn garment in the middle of his field. Maybe he had a clue, living so close to the border. It had to register yet: We were in the West.

We had the shakes from nervous exhaustion and were dying of thirst. We wandered about the deserted city until we found a water tap in a construction site, had our fill and tried to sleep in the dirt until dawn. I found the railway station easy enough and bought tickets to Trieste with our convertible dinars. The ride was Lily's thrilling introduction to Italy. A fast, comfortable, clean train, running high above the ink blue Adriatic, thundering through neat little towns, skirting winding roads filled with nice cars, many pleasure boats criss-crossing the azure waves below. This was what I had preached to her about.

On arrival, we surrendered ourselves to the first policeman at the railway station. He was friendly, which to her was incredible. We had our ingrained fear of police. Especially me, who encountered literally the jackboot of communism.

Here was a handsome, easy-going man, taking us to the Headquarters. Apparently this was no news to them; a daily occurrence: desperate, lost refugees looking for help. In the Prefettura they seated us in a dining room and ordered food from a nearby restaurant. The heaping plate of spaghetti they served felt like the food of the gods. We even got a glass of red wine.

The tiredness, sleeplessness, the extreme nervous tension of the past two nights almost bowled me over. We both lost about ten pounds during the crossing. As we were transported uphill to our camp, I fell into a detached, buoyant golden daze, knowing deep down that something fundamentally great happened to us.

From then on, we were refugees. The familiar complex of concrete barracks in the village of Padriciano was our first "home". As a married couple, we got our own private room, a great improvement over the crowded dormitories of the single guys of the last time. The place was still full of fellow desperados from behind the Iron Curtain: Polish, Czech, Romanian nationals, all happy to be out of their respective Workers Paradises. Also many Hungarians. We developed a quick camaraderie with them which eased the shock of camp life and the immersion into a new world. This was so much better, with Lily at my side.

Some of the tales of escape were beyond belief: what people would do to get to freedom. One guy pushed his wife across a bay, five kilometres of Adriatic Sea from the Yugoslav side to the Italian, at night, on an air mattress. She couldn't swim. One other story was even more daring. They brought their Skoda car with them. A sloping road led to a remote border crossing hut. It was the middle of the night: the barrier was down, locked, the two guards sleeping inside. They cut the engine, slowly rolled to the building. After some measuring, they very quietly unbolted the counterweight of the barrier inches from the guards snoring inside. There was just enough space between the building and the remainder of the bar to squeeze the car through, ever so slowly, inch by inch, since the cheaply made car's brakes were squealing. Meanwhile the guards kept sleeping. Once farther down they started the engine up and rolled to freedom.

In the camp the food was awful: it was poor quality besides being strange to our taste buds. The rooms were bug infested, our movements restricted. But we had hope. It was a sunshine-y,   blue sky kind of glorious hope.

One day the loudspeaker called my name, to go to the administration office. A police officer showed me a chair. He took out of a filing cabinet something frighteningly familiar: my old ID booklet. As there was a language barrier, he called in one of the refugees who spoke Italian to translate.

"How come you are here again? Where have you been for the past two years? Did you go back to Hungary?"

"I went back for my girlfriend."

"For your girlfriend ???" I could see the translator had to repeat the answer twice. It sure sounded unbelievable.

"Why didn't the girlfriend came out with you? How did you manage not to get caught going back?"

"I was lucky. The Hungarians are very inefficient. I made up a story"

"And how come you could get out of Hungary again?"

"Once I convinced my girlfriend to escape with me, we applied for permits . We had to wait a year. This is the truth"

All the awkward, justified questions and all my hard-to-believe answers. He looked sceptical, and he said he had to make a report of this to Interpol and to NATO Intelligence. Next a woman came in and took my fingerprints, which I submitted myself with great reluctance. And I thought I was Scot free with my new papers.

I didn't hear from them after this, not until I tried to immigrate to the States from another camp.

We started the slow process of application. My old army buddy, Laszlo was already in New York, had a job and an apartment and he urged us to get there quickly.

As Padriciano was only a transit camp, we were shipped south to a place called Capua. In the outskirts was our next "home", a former Second World War POW camp. The place made Padriciano look like Club Med. Rows of decrepit sunken huts spread out in a dusty, weed choked compound, full of forlorn, aimlessly loitering refugees. We stuck together with our fellow Hungarians, moving next to each other. The communal toilet had no doors, most of them were used up as firewood in winters before. The wealthy refugees had their own toilet doors, which they carried with them, hung it up while doing their business and carried back into their locked rooms. Once the refugee left, he/she sold the doors to the next family who could afford it.

Security was non-existent. The Carabinieri were afraid to come into the camp. They only manned the useless gate, since the fences were trampled down in many places. While we were there, we woke up one night to a phalanx of heavily armed police advancing through the camp, looking for a demented refugee (there were many there, the ones who never got accepted to any country and rotted their life away in this hellhole) who shot dead one of our fellow Hungarians. He was caught cowering in a cellar, and was taken to an insane asylum.

The constant danger, alien surroundings, the ambiguity of the future brought us even closer with Lily. In town she attracted an unwelcome attention with her looks, sometimes returning to camp with a convoy of Italian cars following her, shaking fistful of liras at her:

"Signorina, quanta costa?"

"Che bella , ecco cinque mille lire. Amore mio"

The locals were convinced that all "profughi" women were available, as unfortunately many were.

But we also had some fun times. Our parties lasted well into the night, and it was my duty- since I owned a decrepit bicycle- to wobble my drunken self through the dark dirt road to town, wake up some unhappy fruit vendor and buy more birra.

Eventually I found some low-paying, exploitative work in the camp. It allowed us to buy edible food and cook it ourselves. I quickly rose to a position of assistant to the big boss, Signor Capasso, who was in charge of room and furniture distributions to everybody. I had a key to the storage rooms, so naturally we had clean linen and the best furniture. Many unfortunate single women earned their way by prostitution. They smuggled the Johns (or Giovannis) into their rooms. Capasso overlooked this because they paid him back in kind. My frequent duty was to put a big padlock outside a door of one of the girls' room, thus locking Capasso and her inside for an hour and unlock it for them after, giving an all clear signal first. Capasso was after all a respected husband and father of three children.

I could've had my reward from these women too, since they constantly begged me for more clean linen, and promising proper payment. Knowing and assisting the bastard Capasso gave me power too and the much needed feeling of superiority: I could get the best rooms for our friends, the best furniture or even a new toilet door. He couldn't object, could he? My dear Lily, who never had to learn to cook, bravely tackled the concept of dinner every night and she quickly acquired the skills of an honourable housewife.

Later Lily also landed an enviable job: a receptionist in a used car dealership in Aversa, a nearby town. The fact that she didn't speak Italian, and couldn't type was no impediment. All the sleazy car salesman wanted was for her is to sit at the front window and look pretty. She was a bait for horny car buyers. The Southern Italians were a sexually oppressed lot in the 1970s. You got laid if you got married or if you hired one of the cheap hookers lining the roads. There was no pre-marital sex unless you were ready to face the shotgun of an enraged father.

She sometimes brought coffee to them, the only work she performed there. Of course they made passes at her, but she kept her distance from them with her usual regal detachment. As an added benefit, they took us out to dinners, dances, movies. I was the necessary baggage they had to carry with them.

We applied as refugees to the US Consulate in Naples. One day I heard my name called on the loudspeaker. In the camp office they informed me that I have to travel to Naples to the American Consulate for an interview. This didn't bode well for me. Nobody ever got called in to Naples. It had to do something with my double escape.

I took a bus on the designated day to the city, leaving the worried Lily behind. I found my way to the Consulate after much wanderings but right on time. An immaculately attired marine with a ridiculous haircut escorted me to a small office. Richard Nixon's mug was the only decoration on the wall. Soon a middle aged woman and a young crew cut in a suit walked in. The matron introduced herself as the translator, a Hungarian living in Naples. The guy must had been CIA, he looked the part. Without much preamble, the man started questioning me in rapid-fire English, the matron translating effectively.

"Why did you go back to Hungary after successfully escaping?"

"How could you go back without papers and never been found out?"

"How come you were issued another ID book?"

"How come you got the permit to leave again?" The same questions like in Padriciano again, but this time with the ferocity of a believer of my treachery.

I kept telling the sceptical man the truth, unbelievable as it sounded. This was a last hurdle I had to mount. After all I went through, right at the threshold of the Promised Land, they try to trip me up. It was difficult to truly relay my emotions through the filter of translation. I resorted to begging: please understand, I just went back to get my girlfriend. The only way I was never found out was because the system in Hungary is so inefficient. I could see my desperate plea had no effect on the young man.

"We'll let you know in a couple of weeks" all he said, standing up and letting us out of the office. I said goodbye to the not-too-friendly translator and exited the Consulate in a turbulent mood.

The waiting in limbo seemed interminable, but eventually the day came when I was called in to the camp office and was informed that my refugee application was rejected. Lily was free to go if she wanted. This was a big blow. My friend Laszlo has already secured a job for me in New York. An appeal, most likely rejected, would bring months of camp-living and more uncertainty to our lives. Dejected, gloomy days followed, not seeing a way out. Our minds were so set on America, we never contemplated any other options. Now we had to. There were only five countries accepting refugees: The States, Canada, Australia, Sweden and South Africa. The Great North of Canada looked like the best bet. To our limited knowledge, this was a peaceful country, not like the turbulent US with the Vietnam War, the riots, assassinations, protests. In hindsight, their rejection was a blessing, landing us in our beloved new country.

To apply to Canada, we had to change camps. We said our good byes to our new friends, packed up our few possessions and took a train to Latina. This was a more civilized camp, within the city, with habitable buildings. We were facing a new environment, new faces and an unknown future. As we came to expect it by now, nothing came easily for us. As soon as we put our papers through to the Canadian embassy, word came of the October Crisis, the killing of a minister by the FLQ. State of Emergency was declared. Immigration was suspended indefinitely. Winter came. We had to find a job to buy warm clothes. Through a delightful Chech friend Lily landed herself a job mending burlap sacks in a feed depot, working standing up in a cold yard for eight hours, sewing patches on an industrial machine. This was a piecework job, so she drove herself very hard. The owners' son picked her up every morning in his Lancia sports car, convincing wagging tongues of the camp of a job other than sewing. We didn't care. She made good money, we had no expenses, so we went to Rome and bought nice clothes to the envy of those tongues.

I quickly learned basic, pidgin Italian. I had an occasional translating job in the offices of the various refugee agencies. The payment for these services were usually drinks in the camp cantina. My dear Lily, coming home dead tired, frequently found me happily ensconced in the bar, in the middle of drunk Hungarians.

Christmas came in the strange land, our second together. We bought a little tree, decorations, presents, Lily cooked special food. We made it the best we could. But the uncertainty of the future constantly gnawed at our insides. Finally we were called in for an interview with the Canadian officials. Medical examinations followed, and on a wonderful day in March we were informed that we were accepted as refugees to Canada. We were in euphoria. The gates to a new life were thrown open.

The day came when we said our goodbyes again and boarded a bus to Rome. They put us up in a cheap hotel of dubious quality for a night. Standing at the window, watching the hookers warming themselves by fire under doorways across the street, I knew I was leaving the first half of my life behind. The umbilical cord tying us to Europe and the life we knew will be ripped apart. But I felt I was ready, confident to face the unknown with Lily by my side. We went to bed but I didn't sleep much that night, our last one on the Old Continent.

Fiumicino airport impressed us, a futuristic space befitting for us space travellers to a new world. This was our first flight, of course. In those innocent, easygoing days we boarded the plane straight out of the waiting area. No baggage screening, body scans, bag searches, shoe removal, liquid confiscations.

Nervously sitting in my seat, belted in, suddenly the plane started to move. We bounced for a long time on the taxiway, and eventually we alighted on the endless looking runway. There were tense moments, the engines roaring, and suddenly the brakes were released. We jumped ahead, pinning my frightened self to my seat. Buildings rushed by in dizzying speed, and then we were air born. The city flew away from us in a reverse zoom action. The clanging of the running gear locking into place gave my heart another lurch. We climbed into clouds, suddenly the world disappeared. We were buffeted violently, making me break out in cold sweat. One of our fellow refugees made good use of her barf bag. We clawed our hands together, ready to die together. But eventually we broke through the gloom to a brilliant sunshine, a snowfield of white clouds spreading forever, the plane coasting smoothly.

This is it, I thought. It was all worth it. We were on our way, our future looming over the horizon at the end of the rainbow.

CPSIA information can be obtained at www.ICGtesting.com
Printed in the USA
LVOW04s2225041114

411987LV00018B/825/P